T0304961

THE
MYTHOLOGY
PUZZLE BOOK

THE MYTHOLOGY PUZZLE BOOK

Copyright © Octopus Publishing Group Limited, 2024

Compiled by Emma Marriott

An Hachette UK Company
www.hachette.co.uk

Summersdale Publishers
Part of Octopus Publishing Group Limited
Carmelite House
50 Victoria Embankment
LONDON
EC4Y 0DZ
UK

www.summersdale.com

Printed and bound in Poland

ISBN: 978-1-83799-162-4

THE
MYTHOLOGY
PUZZLE BOOK

 200 BRAIN-TEASING
ACTIVITIES

FRANCIS NIGHTINGALE

summersdale

INTRODUCTION

Myths are stories that attempt to answer the big questions about life, death and the world around us. Featuring a fantastic array of creatures, gods and heroes, they are as popular today as they were thousands of years ago.

The activities featured in this book will take you on a journey through mythologies found across the world, from the epics of ancient Greece to tales of Aboriginal Dreamtime. Along the way, you'll be teased and tested by a range of puzzles, including crosswords, sudokus and anagrams, as well as riddles and trivia questions that will challenge and maybe even enlighten you!

So, if the names Zeus or Athena ring a bell, or you want to know more about screaming banshees or the Jade Emperor, then why not give these puzzles a go? Packed with 200 games, brainteasers and a host of fun facts, this book promises hours of fun – welcome to the wondrous world of mythology.

1

WORD SEARCH: KING GILGAMESH

Gilgamesh is a mythological king of ancient Mesopotamia, a region in present-day Iraq. The king's quest for eternal life is told in the *Epic of Gilgamesh*. Find the words relating to the poem in the grid.

```
B  D  D  F  S  W  M  G  T  V  O  W  F  D  P
T  A  O  M  Z  S  V  A  N  U  I  V  H  Y  D
L  A  B  U  D  I  K  N  E  T  U  Y  Z  R  N
U  A  H  Y  H  B  K  O  P  T  D  K  E  Z  W
P  M  J  R  L  S  D  B  R  H  T  A  J  A  W
Z  R  C  V  H  O  R  P  E  V  M  N  B  W  H
O  L  D  F  D  U  N  N  S  I  U  R  U  K  R
K  M  G  O  Z  G  O  H  M  O  R  V  L  N  A
Q  M  W  U  O  N  J  K  S  E  Q  V  L  Z  B
X  D  J  W  C  L  O  F  M  Y  Z  C  A  B  S
H  R  T  O  B  C  F  U  D  K  U  Q  N  A  H
G  Q  N  U  G  F  S  S  T  R  U  M  P  F  W
V  X  J  Z  M  Y  K  D  N  D  T  Q  J  K  N
H  N  M  W  I  G  I  Q  M  U  N  N  Z  Y  J
O  D  M  B  A  A  K  Z  U  Q  W  H  L  M  Z
```

ANU	DREAM	SERPENT
BABYLON	ENKIDU	SUMER
BULL	FLOOD	URUK

CROSSWORD: MYTHICAL CREATURES

ACROSS

2. One-eyed giant with enormous strength (7)

5. Has the upper body of a human and the torso and legs of a horse (7)

6. Water-dwelling woman with the tail of a fish (7)

DOWN

1. Lives in caves or on mountains / To deliberately upset someone online (5)

3. Large bird said to be reborn from the ashes of fire (7)

4. Giant, fire-breathing reptile (6)

TRIVIA

In Celtic mythology, how does the frightening female spirit, known as a banshee, signal approaching death?

a) She appears dressed in a black hooded shroud
b) She howls and makes terrifying screams
c) She is accompanied by the sound of a tolling bell

PAIRS GAME

Match up the 20 Greek busts in 20 seconds. The first one has been done for you.

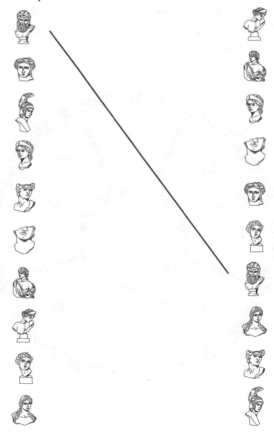

WORD WHEEL

See how many words of four or more letters you can make from the letters below. All words must include the central letter and, apart from the target word, proper nouns don't count! Can you find the name of the Greek goddess of love and beauty that uses all nine letters?

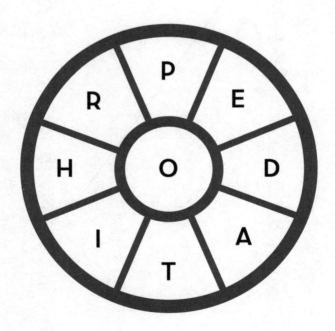

MAZE

Can you help the Greek mythological hero Theseus find his way through the labyrinth to slay the Minotaur?

ANAGRAMS: CHINESE NEW YEAR CELEBRATIONS

In China there is a popular myth about a ferocious beast called Nian who attacked villagers at the beginning of each year. To scare him away they burned lanterns, made loud noises and put up red paper decorations. Rearrange these letters to reveal items often seen at Chinese New Year.

LEN RANT

ERICK FARCER

FERRIS WOK

RON DAG

WORD LADDER

In this word ladder, change one letter at a time to turn the word "fire" into "bull", both of which feature in Greek mythology, such as the Cretan Bull and the god Prometheus, who gave fire to humankind.

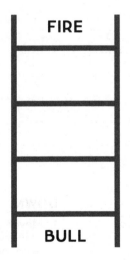

FIRE

BULL

CROSSWORD: MYTHOLOGICAL MOUNTAINS

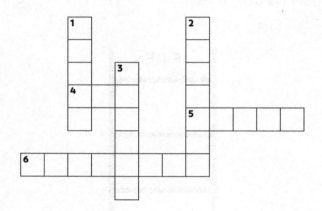

ACROSS:

4. Incan gods or spirits of mountains (3)

5. Figure from a Chinese creation myth whose spine became the mountains (5)

6. Mountains in New South Wales named after the protagonists of an Aboriginal myth, The Three _____ (8)

DOWN:

1. Mayan god who gave maize to humankind by splitting open the mountain where it was hidden (5)

2. Home to the 12 gods of Greek mythology (7)

3. Who in Chinese mythology imprisoned the Monkey King under a mountain? (6)

COUNTING CONUNDRUM

👁 + 👁 + 👁 = 60

👁 + 🧍 + 🧍 = 30

🧍 − 🐍 = 3

👁 + 🧍 + 🐍 = ?

RIDDLE

The following clues will reveal a word used to describe a maiden who, in Norse mythology, guides the souls of those slain in battle to Valhalla.

My first is in raven and also in Venus
My second is in pantheon, but not in fire
My third is in last, but not in fate
My fourth is in wreck and also in kelpie
My fifth is in fairy, but not in fight
My sixth is in water, but not in wail
My seventh is in lion, but not in love
My eighth is in runes, but not in dark

What am I?

WORD SEARCH: HINDU DEITIES

Hinduism has many gods and goddesses who represent different aspects of Brahman, the essence of reality itself. Find the names of other Hindu deities in the grid.

```
H C I R L B Y Q M K X L H B N
M A H V U P P G P N D Q Y X L
J M N F E J K R H P P Z V T Z
F N B U L D U M D Q E D Q U M
C A C Q M U A L W Y C Q U A N
R H U R C A K H Q A I M P I W
N F C I M R N A Z N N I T U
P Y Y E I Q M G B M D D U A I
I M H S K A L T V P R U R V B
S L H A R L W P W H A Z Q R N
K N S A R A S W A T I U P A F
A R E Z O V G A N E S H A P A
Y L H J P Q V I B V B N I T W
V U S O D L Q J X A A T G Y Q
X V S O V T O Z J Y D X T T I
```

GANESHA	**KRISHNA**	**PARVATI**
HANUMAN	**LAKSHMI**	**RAMA**
INDRA	**MAHADEVI**	**SARASWATI**

ACROSTIC

In Roman mythology, Juno cursed the nymph Echo for diverting her while Jupiter was cavorting with other nymphs. Use the clues to find words to write in the grid and the shaded squares will reveal a word meaning preoccupied or unable to concentrate. What is it?

1. Brightly coloured national flower of Mexico
2. Legendary or celebrated
3. Ghost or supernatural being
4. Place of worship
5. State of repugnant, rotting food

1.					
2.					
3.					
4.					
5.					

TRIVIA

The Māori people of New Zealand have many myths relating to the creation of the world, in which the great sky-father and earth-mother, Ranginui and Papatūānuku, play a central role. According to the stories, where were their six sons trapped?

a) In a dark cave filling with sea water
b) In a canoe tossed on the waves in a terrifying storm
c) In the suffocating embrace of their parents

QUIZ: MYSTIFYING WORDS

Here are three words relating to the mythologies of ancient civilizations. Do you have the knowledge to pick the correct definitions?

1. Ziggurat

   a) A symbol associated with the Greek god Zeus
   b) A massive, pyramid-like tower where Mesopotamian gods were worshipped
   c) A Persian god often depicted wielding a large sword

2. Pantheon

   a) A fierce cat-like creature
   b) All the gods of a people or religion
   c) A Greek temple on Mount Olympus

3. Cuneiform

   a) The ancient writing system of Mesopotamia
   b) The voting system in the senate of ancient Athens
   c) A cloven-hoofed messenger god in Greek mythology

SPOT THE
DIFFERENCE

Can you spot the five differences between these two pictures?

WORD BUILDER

The letters of a seven-letter word have been numbered 1 to 7. Use the clues to reveal the name of the Hindu goddess of fertility and fortune, and consort to Vishnu.

Letters 4, 5, 2 and 6 give us a fake

Letters 6, 7, 1 and 3 give us a liquid and source of calcium

Letters 6, 2, 4 and 5 give us a pulp or paste

1	2	3	4	5	6	7

MYSTERY SUDOKU

Complete the grid so that every row, column and 3 × 3 box contains the letters A B E I N O R S W in any order. One row or column contains a seven-letter word that describes what the bridge Bifröst is made of, which in Norse mythology could be used to reach Asgard, the home of the sky gods.

		O	B					E
	E			S		A	B	
	W				E		O	
		N		W		S		
			I		A		N	
		I		B			E	
		S	R		W	N		I
	N						R	

BETWEEN THE LINES

The name of an ancient North African city, ruled by legendary Queen Dido, can be inserted in the blank line so that, reading downwards, eight three-letter words are formed. What is the word hidden between the lines?

A	E	I	S	S	M	A	B
E	R	E	Y	Y	N	E	D

MISSING WORD

On each row of the grid, fill in the blank space to make two compound words or phrases related to mythologies around the world.

Mother		Goddess
Day		Time
Eternal		Force

WORD SEARCH: JAPANESE MYTHS

Japanese mythology contains stories that feature Japan's first emperor, Jimmu, as well as a host of mythical beings. Find the words associated with Japanese mythology in the grid.

```
I  T  V  K  D  Z  B  A  Z  B  M  B  D  I  V
K  M  A  X  Q  M  J  M  E  N  U  S  T  I  K
O  Y  C  N  R  F  F  A  O  I  Z  D  D  W  I
H  Y  F  V  U  G  T  T  V  P  K  W  J  M  W
S  O  K  J  K  K  V  E  V  Z  U  I  A  I  G
N  K  M  F  B  K  I  R  C  S  M  G  J  A  T
O  A  J  C  U  S  E  A  T  M  I  Z  Z  O  Y
H  I  J  G  X  W  C  S  U  K  T  Z  W  A  K
I  O  Q  M  W  S  K  U  I  F  G  P  F  D  S
N  B  Z  B  N  B  F  H  H  S  R  Y  D  X  U
W  A  M  G  Y  A  S  L  U  O  Z  Z  W  L  D
K  E  R  B  H  S  T  W  W  Q  W  Z  L  A  G
S  P  I  R  I  T  S  K  I  T  L  W  D  S  W
E  P  H  I  O  R  Y  B  M  C  Q  P  X  W  Y
Q  R  Y  B  J  V  P  W  J  C  E  B  M  O  Q
```

AMATERASU   KOJIKI   SPIRITS

JIMMU   NIHON SHOKI   TANUKI

KITSUNE   SHIKIGAMI   YOKAI

CROSSWORD: CHARACTERS IN GREEK MYTHOLOGY

ACROSS:

3. She was told never to open that jar (7)

5. He flew too close to the sun (6)

6. Writer of *The Iliad*, the epic poem about the Trojan War (5)

DOWN:

1. Husband of Helen who amassed a Greek army to attack Troy (8)

2. He went in search of the golden fleece (5)

4. Ruler of the underworld (5)

TRIVIA

Mayan mythology, which flourished in Mexico and Central America from around 250 BCE, features a large number of deities. How did the Maya communicate with and appease their gods?

a) With smoke signals
b) Through bloodletting and human sacrifice
c) By consuming fermented beer and hallucinogens

PAIRS GAME

Match up the 20 Celtic symbols in 20 seconds. The first one has been done for you.

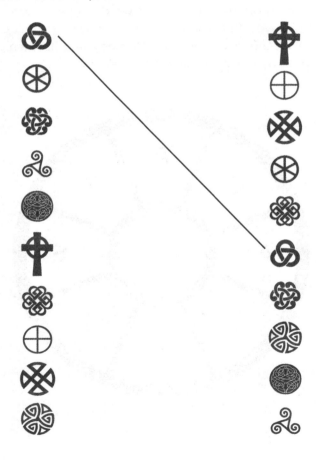

WORD WHEEL

See how many words of four or more letters you can make from the letters below. All words must include the central letter and, apart from the target word, proper nouns don't count! Can you find the name of a region in the Central Pacific that influenced Māori mythology and its themes of travel and water, which uses all nine letters?

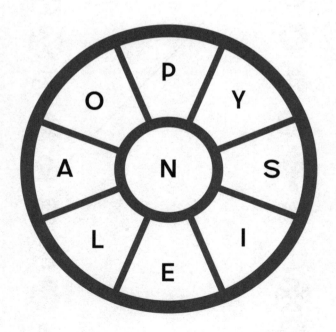

MAZE

Can you help the Aboriginal deity, the Rainbow Serpent, find her way out of the maze to her home, the waterhole?

ANAGRAMS: SCANDINAVIAN SAGAS

Rearrange the letters to reveal words often associated with Norse myths.

AGSA

MAHMRE

RIOWARR

USREN

WORD LADDER

In this word ladder, change one letter at a time to turn the word "moon" into "hare", a symbol of good fortune in Celtic mythology.

MOON

HARE

CROSSWORD: WORDS DERIVED FROM THE NAMES OF GREEK DEITIES

ACROSS:

2. The favourite drink of gods and goddesses (6)

5. Sleep-like state of consciousness (8)

6. Name of the god condemned to carry the heavens on his shoulders (5)

DOWN:

1. Archenemy or villain (7)

3. Irrational fear (6)

4. Primordial goddess, the very first entity in existence (5)

COUNTING CONUNDRUM

🔑 + 🔑 + 🔑 = 45

🔑 + 🐱 + 🐱 = 35

🐱 − 👁 = 8

🔑 + 🐱 + 👁 = ?

WORD LINK

The three words in each of the clues below have another word in common. For example, if the clue included the words "count", "faith" and "weight", the answer would be "lose" (lose count, lose faith and lose weight). Write the answers in the grid to reveal a word in the shaded column that is the name of a large Greek island and home to King Minos.

1. Cherry, ice, tooth

2. Loser, point, throat

3. Bird, pod, money

4. Rug, bubble, salts

5. Pressure, group, review

1.			
2.			
3.			
4.			
5.			

WORD SEARCH: THE AZTECS

The city of Tenochtitlan, now Mexico City, is said to have been built on the spot where travellers spotted an eagle perched on a cactus, holding a rattlesnake. Find the words associated with Aztec mythology in the grid.

T	Q	Q	F	T	P	N	M	X	M	J	C	M	U	J
E	N	M	F	E	K	A	N	S	E	L	T	T	A	R
S	A	E	J	G	W	B	N	F	X	H	X	S	Q	D
G	V	G	P	H	J	T	T	X	I	D	A	U	N	O
Z	H	D	L	R	J	T	X	Z	C	N	E	A	S	G
F	T	C	U	E	E	L	X	H	O	T	L	K	E	N
C	A	C	T	U	S	S	G	K	Z	T	P	J	W	U
T	O	N	A	T	I	U	H	A	I	S	V	K	L	S
V	X	Q	Z	C	Z	D	L	T	J	D	V	T	K	W
J	C	W	A	O	I	C	H	H	M	V	T	M	U	H
I	T	G	F	Y	O	C	H	E	D	Z	E	M	C	Y
K	V	R	M	A	O	Y	H	G	T	M	T	Z	O	B
P	A	O	T	N	Q	U	O	X	U	C	Q	L	W	C
J	V	L	E	E	Q	K	T	T	H	S	Q	J	R	K
Q	B	T	N	Q	P	K	O	D	D	A	E	H	G	T

CACTUS	QUETZALCOATL	SUN GOD
EAGLE	RATTLESNAKE	TENOCHTITLAN
MEXICO	SERPENT	TONATIUH

ACROSTIC

Use the clues to find words to write in the grid and the shaded squares will reveal a ten-letter word meaning the final destruction of the world, known in Hindu mythology as Kali Yuga. What is it?

1. Descend using rope

2. Remove contaminants

3. Supplies lubricant to a machine

4. Plants that produce sour fruit

5. Guidance or recommendation

1.					
2.					
3.					
4.					
5.					

TRIVIA

According to Japanese mythology, where was Princess Kaguya found when she was a baby?

a) In a giant spiderweb
b) On the shores of a lake
c) Inside a bamboo stalk

QUIZ: ROMAN DEITIES

Like the ancient Greeks, people in the Roman world worshipped multiple gods and goddesses. Can you match the description with the correct god?

1. **Queen of the gods**
   a) Juno
   b) Minerva
   c) Diana

2. **Goddess of agriculture, the harvest and the seasons**
   a) Venus
   b) Vesta
   c) Ceres

3. **Messenger of the gods and god of travellers and commerce**
   a) Mercury
   b) Neptune
   c) Mars

SPOT THE
DIFFERENCE

Can you spot the five differences between these two pictures?

WORD BUILDER

The letters of a seven-letter word have been numbered 1 to 7. Use the clues to reveal the name of the many-armed, elephant-headed god in Hindu mythology.

Letters 6, 7, 3 and 1 give us a way to suspend something

Letters 2, 5 and 6 give us a product of fire

Letters 5, 2, 3 and 4 give us the opposite of mad

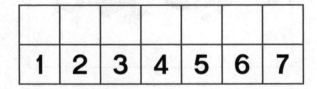

38

MYSTERY SUDOKU

Complete the grid so that every row, column and 3 × 3 box contains the letters A B C L O P S T Y in any order. One row or column contains a seven-letter word that is the name of the nymph who kept Greek hero Odysseus on her island, as well as a type of West Indian music.

			A	L				
		T			P	A		
A	Y						S	
		A					L	
O	S							C
T	L							O
		L			T		C	
Y			L	S		B		
	P		B	A		T		

BETWEEN THE LINES

The name for the apocalypse in Norse mythology can be inserted in the blank line so that, reading downwards, eight three-letter words are formed. What is the word hidden between the lines?

T	C	A	A	M	C	S	S
Y	R	E	T	P	Y	N	Y

HIDDEN WORDS

In each of the sentences below, one of the 12 animals that make up the Chinese zodiac is hidden. For instance, in the sentence "I left my car at the airport", the word "rat" is hidden in "ca**r at**".

1. Did you see the flamingo at the lake?
2. A Christmas tree looks naked without decorations.
3. Adding avocado gives the recipe colour and vibrancy.
4. Witnesses in the restaurant saw a dog grab bits of food from people's plates.
5. The icy landscape was full of enormous, deep igloos glinting in the sun.

WORD SEARCH: CHEEKY MONKEY

Sun Wukong, also known as the Monkey King, is a Chinese trickster god. Find the words relating to this famous character in the grid.

```
Y G W Y K C Z T M V B Y W P E
P T O J G I O P S J E M L B G
Y E I U N G R D E K O J Y C D
E A A L Y A R N N A C O V W X
B N A C A M U O T K B G H L L
X M R O H T M L I S P C F K Q
S R U X Z E R M O U N T A I N
U Y A N T E S O G N I K B Q X
N X K U S R F V M W K U K U W
W M B P U V N P C M D Z A O T
U F J L Y X S H T D I N T I F
K R V S X F K X H G Z B E T S
O S J Z C E V A O A P Z L O T
N H Z X K N A A N O N N R M C
G I R A E A U G N E H A E C S
```

BUDDHA	MAGIC	PEACHES
KING	MONKEY	SUN WUKONG
IMMORTALITY	MOUNTAIN	XUANZANG

CROSSWORD: SACRED CITIES

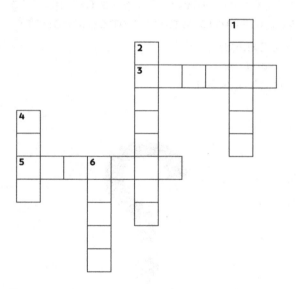

ACROSS:

3. Named after the Greek goddess of wisdom (6)

5. Founded by Perseus (7)

DOWN:

1. Established by Brutus the Trojan, after defeating two ancient British giants (6)

2. Founded by the Hindu god Shiva and now a place of pilgrimage in India (7)

4. Founded by Romulus and Remus on the site where they were suckled by a she-wolf (4)

6. Sumerian city and home to god Enki (5)

TRIVIA

The tragic tale of the Children of Lir in Celtic mythology is thought to have inspired which famous ballet?

a) *La Sylphide*
b) *Swan Lake*
c) *The Nutcracker*

PAIRS GAME

Match up the 20 Aztec symbols in 20 seconds. The first one has been done for you.

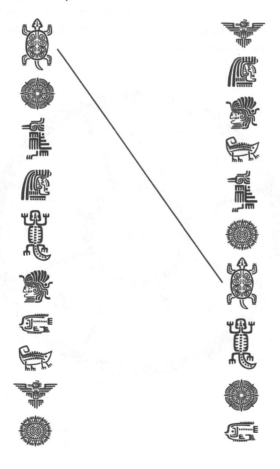

WORD WHEEL

See how many words of four or more letters you can make from the letters below. All words must include the central letter and, apart from the target word, proper nouns don't count! Can you find the nine-letter word for the family who lived on Mount Olympus?

MAZE

Can you help the villagers escape Nian, the Chinese man-eating beast with a lion's head?

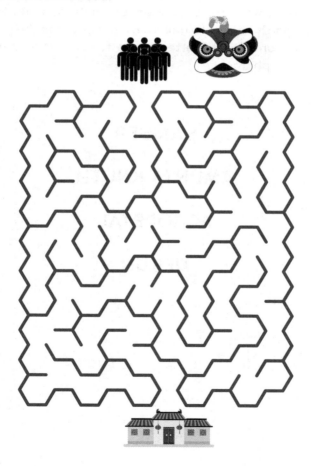

ANAGRAMS: EGYPTIAN RULERS

In Egyptian mythology, the ancient pharaohs were considered gods on earth, chosen to maintain order and lead the people. Can you rearrange the letters below to reveal the names of well-known pharaohs?

SAMSER

AMUNTA KNUTH

ACROPETAL

UFKUH

48

WORD LADDER

Greek hero Odysseus instructed his crew to plug their ears with beeswax so that they wouldn't hear the song of the sirens, who would otherwise lure them to their deaths. Change "sing" into "rule" by altering one letter at a time to make a new word on each step of the ladder.

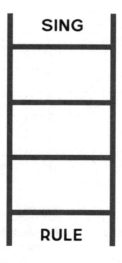

SING

RULE

CROSSWORD: MYTHOLOGICAL NORSE BEASTS

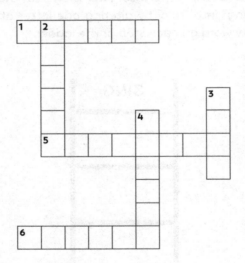

ACROSS:

1. Ugly creatures who lived underground or on mountains or forests (6)

5. A creature that ran up and down the sacred tree, Yggdrasil (8)

6. Known as Nidhogg, an enormous beast with claws, scales and horns (6)

DOWN:

2. Called Huggin and Muninn, these two black birds were the helpers of the supreme god, Odin (6)

3. Known as Fenrir, a terrifying creature who will break free of his chains when the apocalypse comes (4)

4. A famous sea monster so large that people mistook it for an island (6)

COUNTING CONUNDRUM

🏺 + 🏺 + 🏺 = 54

🏺 + 🏺 + 🏛 = 45

🏛 − 🗿 = 4

🏺 + 🏛 + 🗿 = ?

RIDDLE

The following clues will reveal a word that means a communal celebration, many of which have origins in myth.

My first is in elf and also in fire
My second is in beast, but not in boast
My third is in wish, but not in wreck
My fourth is in trick and also in feast
My fifth is in fairy, but not in fear
My sixth is in weave, but not in wonder
My seventh is in star, but not in sun
My eighth is in fly, but not in ogre

What am I?

WORD SEARCH: THE TITANS

In Greek mythology, the original 12 Titan gods were six brothers and six sisters. Find nine of these gods in the grid.

X	D	J	T	Y	C	Y	I	C	V	J	H	U	J	B
I	R	O	V	F	R	C	L	C	O	Y	C	Y	Y	Y
W	M	Q	H	U	I	O	O	W	P	E	H	P	S	M
K	Y	X	Z	A	U	Q	C	E	L	W	U	Y	Z	W
U	I	N	H	E	S	D	R	E	Y	D	H	S	Q	W
R	S	Y	P	H	G	I	S	X	A	T	U	U	Q	B
I	M	A	H	R	O	E	L	X	E	N	M	D	M	E
C	V	H	Y	N	O	V	B	T	B	Q	U	M	J	Y
B	K	S	Z	O	D	B	Z	E	V	M	M	S	M	G
W	R	O	X	U	N	O	G	H	O	K	E	W	Q	L
M	Q	R	M	S	T	J	Y	P	V	H	Z	N	K	G
Q	F	R	O	S	U	T	E	P	A	I	P	N	C	J
T	H	E	M	I	S	Q	J	T	K	G	U	X	Q	M
M	X	P	S	S	W	Y	M	W	W	X	G	P	R	A
T	P	Q	B	M	Z	I	U	U	A	N	Y	O	M	N

COEUS	IAPETUS	RHEA
CRIUS	OCEANUS	TETHYS
HYPERION	PHOEBE	THEMIS

53

ACROSTIC

Use the clues to find words to write in the grid and the shaded squares will reveal a ten-letter word meaning overwhelming distress, particularly in matters of love, such as in the Greek myth of star-crossed lovers Pyramus and Thisbe. What is it?

1. Noise and chatter made by a crowd of people

2. Used to rub something out

3. Suggest or recommend

4. Layer at the back of the eyeball sensitive to light

5. Official currency of Mongolia

1.					
2.					
3.					
4.					
5.					

TRIVIA

According to Celtic mythology, how does the warrior hero Fionn mac Cumhaill call upon the wisdom of the salmon of knowledge?

a) By playing a magical flute
b) By washing his feet
c) By sucking his thumb

QUIZ: MESOAMERICAN GODS

How well do you know the mythologies of the Mayan, Aztec and Incan civilizations? Do you have the knowledge to identify the correct descriptions?

1. **Kukulkan, the Mayan creator god, was often depicted as:**

   a) A feathered serpent
   b) A woman with jaguar ears
   c) An eagle

2. **Which Aztec god is closely related to the Mayan god Kukulkan?**

   a) Tlaloc
   b) Quetzalcoatl
   c) Tezcatlipoca

3. **Which Incan god was the goddess of grain and corn?**

   a) Kon
   b) Illapa
   c) Mama Sara

SPOT THE DIFFERENCE

Can you spot the five differences between these two pictures?

WORD BUILDER

The letters of a seven-letter word have been numbered 1 to 7. Use the clues to reveal the name of a Roman goddess.

Letters 6, 2, 3 and 4 give us the stem of a climbing plant

Letters 1, 7 and 3 give us the opposite of a woman

Letters 5, 2 and 1 give us the outer edge of a circular object

Letters 5, 7, 6 and 4 give us a word meaning to talk about something incoherently or with great enthusiasm

1	**2**	**3**	**4**	**5**	**6**	**7**

MYSTERY SUDOKU

Complete the grid so that every row, column and 3 × 3 box contains the letters A E I J P R S T U in any order. One row or column contains a seven-letter word that is the name of the king of the Roman gods, and god of the sky and thunder.

		E			P			
J			I					
		R	A	U		I		
		U			T		E	
	E	A				S	T	
	J		U			A		
		S		I	A	E		
				R				A
			T			J		

BETWEEN THE LINES

The name of a forebear from whom someone is descended, such as Saturn, grandfather of Juventas in Roman mythology, can be inserted in the blank line so that, reading downwards, eight three-letter words are formed. What is the hidden word between the lines?

S	A	I	P	A	S	G	O
D	T	E	T	K	Y	D	B

MISSING WORD

Mythologies around the world feature the vast oceans of our planet, which are ruled over by a variety of different gods, from Tangaroa in Māori myth to Mama Qucha, the Incan goddess of the sea. On each line of the grid, fill in the blank space to make two compound words or phrases that are related to the sea or ocean.

Flying		Bone
Deep		Monster
Tidal		Length

WORD SEARCH: DREAMTIME

Aboriginal Dreamtime is the era in which the world was created, as well as a world view encompassing morals and humanity's relationship with the natural environment. Find these words associated with Dreamtime in the grid.

N	D	A	A	U	I	S	X	A	O	Q	R	U	N	V
T	Y	R	T	Z	K	H	L	G	S	L	G	W	B	Z
S	R	O	T	S	E	C	N	A	J	L	S	T	S	F
S	K	C	A	R	T	I	L	W	M	O	M	T	E	M
Q	F	F	N	P	M	D	P	F	N	I	L	X	R	W
Q	D	M	B	A	P	N	J	G	Y	S	N	S	P	Y
S	K	M	E	C	B	O	L	W	A	L	C	A	E	N
S	U	R	T	B	N	I	R	K	W	A	T	I	N	Y
D	D	F	L	U	N	T	B	A	S	K	P	F	T	B
W	E	B	I	E	O	A	T	E	I	A	N	I	N	K
T	U	Y	S	T	Q	E	L	G	K	N	E	E	D	N
G	A	T	C	F	Q	R	B	F	Q	B	B	T	S	O
A	L	A	X	M	S	C	I	N	S	O	C	O	I	U
E	G	B	Z	M	H	C	I	O	Q	E	R	S	W	C
L	A	N	D	S	C	A	P	E	X	H	J	V	K	X

ANCESTORS   DREAMING   RAINBOW

ANIMALS   LANDSCAPE   SONGLINES

CREATION   SERPENT   TRACKS

CROSSWORD: IN THE BEGINNING

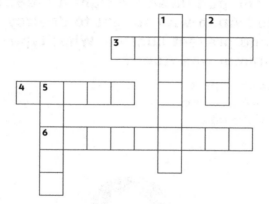

ACROSS:

3. Creator god in Hinduism who emerges out of chaos and darkness (6)

4. In Chinese mythology, this giant used his own body to create the world (5)

6. A creator ancestor of the Kaurna people in Aboriginal mythology (9)

DOWN:

1. In Greek mythology, she was the first woman on earth (7)

2. A Norse giant made from ice, out of which the world was made (4)

5. Ometeotl was the first deity according to this mythology (5)

63

TRIVIA

In Egyptian mythology, every night
the sun god Ra would fight a creature
called Apep who sought to destroy
Ra and prevent sunrise. What type
of animal was Apep?

a) A serpent
b) A crocodile
c) A beetle

PAIRS GAME

Match up the 20 Greek vases in 20 seconds. The first one has been done for you.

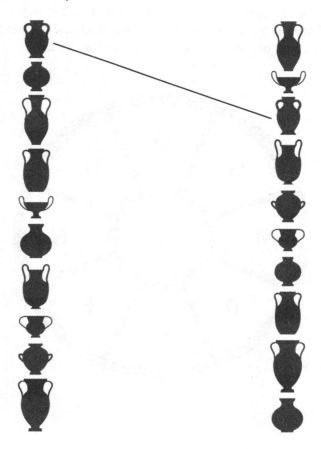

WORD WHEEL

See how many words of four or more letters you can make from the letters below. All words must include the central letter, and proper nouns don't count! Using all the letters, can you find the word used to describe someone who gives their name to a story, such as Odysseus and *The Odyssey*?

MAZE

Can you help the wooden horse, hiding Greek soldiers, get to the gates of Troy?

ANAGRAMS: MAYAN ANIMALS

The Mayans gave religious, mythological and symbolic importance to a variety of animals. Rearrange these letters to reveal animals that often featured in Mayan mythology.

NOLFAC

GURJAA

ALTERNTAKES

MALDOLARI

WORD LADDER

Aurora was the Roman goddess of dawn. Change "dawn" into "life" by altering one letter at a time to make a new word on each step of the ladder.

DAWN

LIFE

CROSSWORD: MYTHOLOGICAL MOVIES

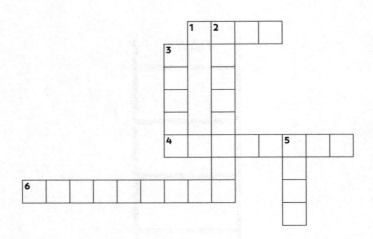

ACROSS:

1. Marvel superhero movie named after the Norse god of thunder (4)

4. Title of a legendary island overwhelmed by the sea (8)

6. *Jason and the _____* (9)

DOWN:

2. Disney movie named after the son of Zeus (8)

3. Sorceress and title of Greek tragedy (5)

5. Brad Pitt plays Achilles in this epic historical adventure (4)

COUNTING CONUNDRUM

owl + owl + owl = 96

owl + owl + flag = 76

flag − ankh = 7

owl + flag + ankh = ?

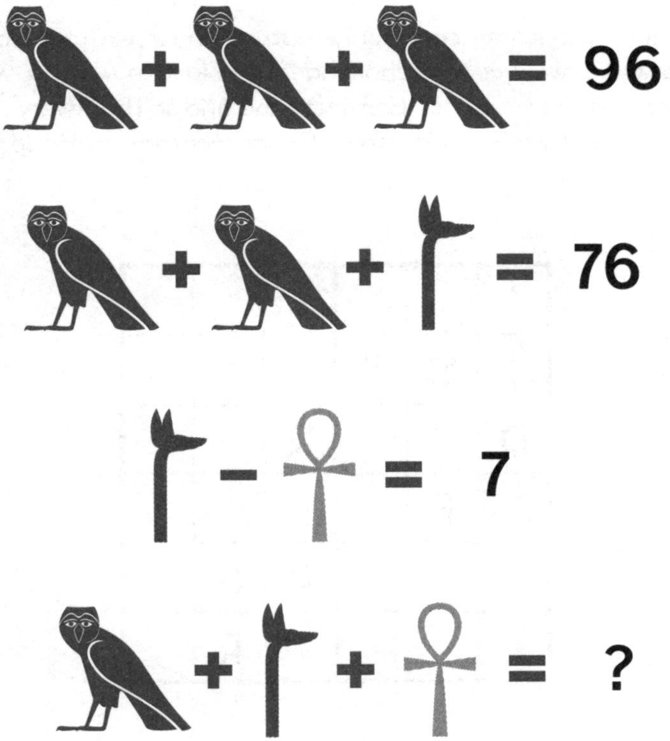

MINI SUDOKU: ARACHNE THE SPIDER

Arachne the spider commonly features in Greek mythology. She was a weaver who challenged and lost to Athena, who turned her into a spider. Complete the grid so that every row, column and 2 × 3 box contains the letters that make up the word "spider".

I					
	S	P			
D			R		
	E				I
			P	S	
				R	

WORD SEARCH: TOO CLOSE TO THE SUN

Find the words associated with the Greek tale of Icarus and Daedalus, his inventor father, in the grid.

F	A	V	I	K	C	F	P	A	N	I	W	R	E	W
E	B	E	P	X	B	X	B	X	C	Q	V	U	T	M
A	D	R	O	W	N	E	D	A	U	O	Y	S	E	Z
T	J	R	A	K	U	E	R	H	G	M	D	X	R	Q
H	F	K	V	A	F	U	S	T	D	O	T	R	C	J
E	U	R	A	D	S	U	X	L	F	J	S	K	Y	P
R	J	N	R	U	L	I	U	A	A	H	W	X	V	V
S	L	K	F	A	S	Q	Z	P	W	B	F	C	Y	X
L	G	A	D	D	E	G	T	T	F	S	I	H	C	X
L	X	E	N	K	W	S	N	Z	S	B	E	S	F	S
S	A	G	S	W	F	F	C	I	N	B	U	E	W	P
D	Z	D	F	P	K	F	D	A	W	N	R	G	B	P
H	V	I	D	E	W	U	J	X	P	H	P	X	K	G
F	U	D	W	L	T	H	X	A	O	E	V	G	H	I
R	S	O	N	I	M	C	M	Q	Y	Y	U	M	G	D

BEESWAX	**DROWNED**	**ICARUS**
CRETE	**ESCAPE**	**MINOS**
DAEDALUS	**FEATHERS**	**WINGS**

ACROSTIC

In Hindu mythology, the character Mahishasura waged war against the gods. Use the clues to find words to write in the grid, and the shaded squares will reveal his true nature. What is it?

1. Anticipate with fear and trepidation

2. Greek soldiers hid in a giant wooden one

3. Imagine while asleep or in a vision

4. Large, thick-skinned animal with one or two horns

5. Belonging to a family of giants in Greek mythology

1.				
2.				
3.				
4.				
5.				

TRIVIA

In Celtic mythology, which creature is often regarded as a symbol of age and wisdom?

a) Hare
b) Eagle
c) Deer

QUIZ: NORSE LEGENDS

1. **Which of the following gods is associated with thunder and lightning in Norse mythology?**
   a) Freya
   b) Loki
   c) Thor

2. **Which realm is the home of the gods?**
   a) Niflheim
   b) Alfheim
   c) Asgard

3. **Which creature is said to herald the onset of Ragnarök?**
   a) Fenrir
   b) Nidhogg
   c) Jörmungandr

SPOT THE DIFFERENCE

Can you spot the five differences between these two pictures?

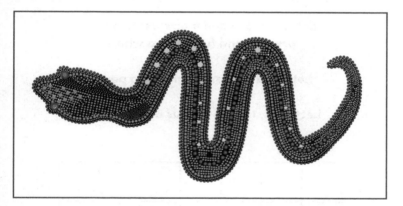

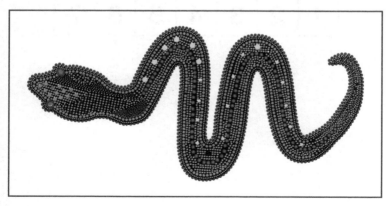

WORD BUILDER

The letters of a seven-letter word have been numbered 1 to 7. Use the clues to reveal the name of the Greek goddess whose golden hind Heracles sought to find.

Letters 3, 6, 5 and 4 give us the past, present and future as a whole

Letters 2, 4, 7 and 3 give us a pause

Letters 2, 1 and 5 give us a male sheep

1	2	3	4	5	6	7

MYSTERY SUDOKU

Complete the grid so that every row, column and 3 × 3 box contains the letters A D E H N P R T U in any order. One row or column contains a seven-letter word for a natural phenomenon associated with the Greek god Zeus.

				P			U	
				U				D
		A	R			T		
	H		U				A	
D		U			E			P
	A	P	D			U		
R			P	E		E		
			N		H			
P			D		R			

BETWEEN THE LINES

Hemera was the Greek and Roman goddess of daylight, and a word meaning daylight can be inserted in the blank line so that, reading downwards, eight three-letter words are formed. What is the word hidden between the lines?

A	F	A	A	S	T	A	B
K	N	D	H	Y	P	Y	E

RIDDLE

The following clues will reveal the name of the Greek god of strength and heroes.

My first is in Athens and also in Thebes
My second is in Eros, but not in star
My third is in war, but not in wound
My fourth is in ocean and also in oar
My fifth is in face, but not in fear
My sixth is in bold, but not in bad
My seventh is in deer, but not in dawn
My eighth is in ask, but not in altar

Who am I?

WORD SEARCH: CELTIC GODS AND HEROES

Find the names of some of these characters in the grid.

A	L	V	O	V	N	B	S	S	X	M	M	P	M	M
Q	D	A	W	T	X	A	R	L	W	C	B	F	A	D
X	G	G	B	L	G	P	S	Z	O	G	E	F	N	M
W	O	B	A	E	U	I	N	A	N	T	W	G	A	Q
T	C	L	N	D	Y	G	C	S	H	S	I	J	N	T
Q	T	I	R	Q	E	E	H	E	M	B	A	B	N	J
G	F	B	B	B	P	H	M	V	G	R	N	A	Á	I
P	K	B	Y	D	E	Ó	T	D	K	E	N	T	N	P
D	O	D	Y	H	R	I	T	D	N	Y	A	U	X	H
L	B	A	P	R	D	B	U	L	L	I	D	S	O
F	R	V	Í	Z	R	H	W	Q	Q	Q	F	O	P	F
P	K	G	C	I	N	N	I	A	L	U	H	C	Ú	C
D	A	I	G	E	C	Z	H	Y	W	K	H	E	H	I
N	Y	I	O	Z	J	F	L	M	L	B	F	J	H	W
N	D	D	P	L	I	R	G	N	O	W	F	B	P	W

BRIGID	FINEGAS	MANANNÁN
CÚ CHULAINN	LIR	THE DAGDA
FIANNA	LUGH	THE MÓRRÍGAN

CROSSWORD: MYSTICAL LANDS

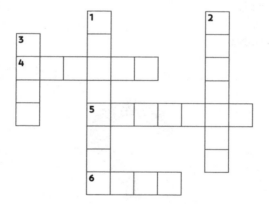

ACROSS:

4. Island featured in the British legend of King Arthur (6)

5. An earthly paradise of ancient Greece (7)

6. Also known as the Field of Reeds, the name for heavenly paradise in Egyptian mythology (4)

DOWN:

1. Hall of slain warriors in Norse mythology (8)

2. In Greek mythology, the final resting place for the souls of the heroic (7)

3. Legendary mountain in Chinese mythology (4)

TRIVIA

Who is the ancient Egyptian god of the afterlife and the judge of souls?

a) Osiris
b) Ra
c) Anubis

PAIRS GAME

Match up the 20 helmets in 20 seconds. The first one has been done for you.

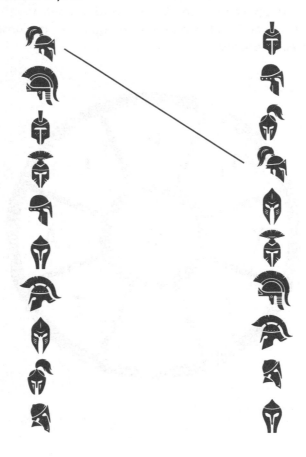

WORD WHEEL

See how many words of four or more letters you can make from the letters below. All words must include the central letter and, apart from the target word, proper nouns don't count! Can you find the name of the queen of the Amazons that uses all the letters?

MAZE

Can you help the pixie, a magical creature from Celtic mythology, find its way to the forest?

ANAGRAMS: THE UNDERWORLD

Rearrange these letters to reveal the names of just some of the characters who live in the underworld of Greek mythology.

SHADE

HEEP PERSON

BE CURSER

ANCHOR

WORD LADDER

Epic poems feature in many bodies of myth, from *The Odyssey* to the *Epic of Gilgamesh*. Change "poem" into "soar" by altering one letter at a time to make a new word on each step of the ladder.

POEM

SOAR

CROSSWORD: SACRED TREES

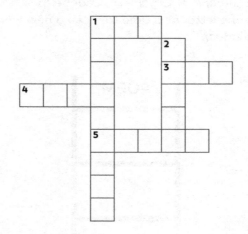

ACROSS:

1. Seen in English churchyards, used as a symbol of immortality in Celtic mythology (3)

3. Often associated with Zeus (3)

4. This body part of Hun Hunahpu was hung in a tree when he was executed by the Lords of Death in Mayan mythology (4)

5. A tree holds the two worlds of the land and the sky apart in this mythology (5)

DOWN:

1. Sacred ash tree of Norse mythology (9)

2. The first man and woman, Ask and Embla, were created from two fallen trees in this mythology (5)

COUNTING CONUNDRUM

(bird) + (bird) + (bird) = 75

(bird) + (bird) + (mask) = 62

(mask) − (dog) = 2

(bird) + (mask) + (dog) = ?

DOWN THE MIDDLE

Complete all the following words correctly to reveal, in the shaded squares, the name of the Egyptian goddess of the dead.

B	E		C	H
E	L		G	Y
P	A		E	R
A	S		E	N
H	O		E	L
O	T		E	R
A	B		S	S
E	A		E	L

WORD SEARCH: THE DAGDA'S HARP

In this Celtic myth, monstrous beings, the Fomorians, stole the Dagda's harp. The Dagda, however, won it back. Find the words associated with the story in the grid.

K	N	J	W	H	D	I	D	T	L	T	F	Y	P	M
T	E	S	V	N	I	I	K	B	S	O	P	R	A	H
C	O	L	U	E	V	P	E	N	M	A	P	L	H	Y
C	I	S	O	U	I	S	B	O	W	W	L	V	M	M
Z	O	S	R	M	N	I	R	N	Y	G	A	B	U	U
V	V	Y	U	T	E	I	I	I	G	D	A	G	N	F
K	Q	S	Z	M	A	C	U	V	G	O	X	E	X	K
R	A	T	D	N	A	Y	K	A	J	D	I	J	B	F
Q	I	F	S	A	Z	I	D	C	A	S	T	L	E	P
H	R	V	U	R	N	E	B	W	E	E	Z	V	V	E
T	C	W	H	Y	H	A	K	P	K	J	E	K	E	E
A	E	L	P	T	E	T	N	Z	P	T	M	X	V	L
T	H	I	E	V	E	S	K	N	X	J	N	U	R	S
C	W	P	H	C	O	F	O	X	Q	W	Q	M	Y	H
U	Q	N	J	F	U	O	Z	R	G	R	Q	L	E	C

CASTLE	FOMORIANS	SLEEP
DANANN	HARP	THE DAGDA
DIVINE	MUSIC	THIEVES

ACROSTIC

Use the clues to find words to write in the grid and the shaded squares will reveal the name of the Titan trickster who stole fire from the hearth of Hephaestus and Athena, only to give it to humans. What is it?

1. A figure controlled by strings
2. Enjoy immensely
3. An angle between 90 and 180 degrees
4. An individual's social background
5. Moral principles

1.					
2.					
3.					
4.					
5.					

TRIVIA

In Celtic mythology, Aoife marries
the husband of her dead sister, Aoibh.
She is jealous of Aoibh's children
and takes them to a lake, planning
to kill them. However, she can't do
the deed but instead transforms
them into something else — can you
identify what?

a) Four mermaids
b) Four swans
c) Four fish

95

QUIZ: PANGU

1. **According to Chinese legend, the first living being, Pangu, separated the opposing forces of yin and yang to create:**
   a) The earth and sky
   b) The sea and land
   c) The sun and moon

2. **When Pangu died, what did his flesh become?**
   a) Rivers
   b) Soil
   c) Precious stones

3. **How is Pangu usually depicted?**
   a) Hairy and humanlike with horns
   b) Half man, half bear
   c) As a monkey

SPOT THE DIFFERENCE

Can you spot the five differences between these two pictures?

WORD BUILDER

The letters of a seven-letter word have been numbered 1 to 7. Use the clues to reveal the name of a lion-headed, fire-breathing Egyptian goddess.

Letters 5, 2, 6 and 3 give us quiet and submissive

Letters 7, 4, 2 and 5 give us a pronoun

Letters 1, 4, 2, 6 and 7 give us a thin, rectangular-shaped object

1	2	3	4	5	6	7

MYSTERY SUDOKU

Complete the grid so that every row, column and 3 × 3 box contains the letters A B E I N Q T U Y in any order. One row or column contains a seven-letter word of which Thalia was the goddess in Greek mythology.

			I				A	
	A	N						
		U						
	I		T				U	A
	B					E		
	N		A				Y	Q
		E			N	Q		T
	Y	B						
			B				N	

BETWEEN THE LINES

A word for a person with wide knowledge or learning, such as Daedalus in Greek mythology, can be inserted in the blank line so that, reading downwards, eight three-letter words are formed. What is the hidden word between the lines?

A	T	S	R	I	B	S	S
E	E	Y	E	P	G	Y	E

CROSS OUT

Cross out all the letters that appear more than once. The letters that are left, reading from top to bottom and left to right, will spell out the word for a male sorcerer, such as Merlin from the mythological stories of King Arthur. What is it?

E	M	T	Y	W	B	J	O
L	O	I	U	N	P	C	Z
J	E	Y	T	U	M	O	A
C	P	R	N	L	D	M	B

WORD SEARCH: PRINCE PWYLL

In Celtic mythology, Pwyll is the Welsh prince of Dyfed. He wins the goddess Rhiannon from a rival, Gwawl, and they have a son, Pryderi. Find the words associated with the story in the grid.

X	N	F	Y	U	N	M	I	Y	W	K	U	X	T	S
E	S	O	Q	N	Y	K	F	X	P	G	Z	E	X	Y
H	U	I	N	C	O	J	F	R	Y	A	Y	M	K	X
W	J	Z	V	N	Y	B	Y	O	H	Q	K	V	W	V
A	I	Y	A	H	A	D	L	Q	D	P	B	A	G	O
Y	P	Q	A	J	E	I	W	E	S	T	G	C	N	A
F	B	N	D	R	W	C	H	R	M	R	J	D	I	R
C	B	T	I	V	C	Y	P	R	N	A	P	K	D	N
K	D	B	Q	E	H	T	R	L	I	Y	N	Q	D	C
L	E	H	Q	S	S	J	I	L	L	Y	W	P	E	W
Z	F	J	M	A	R	I	N	L	R	O	N	F	W	Z
Q	Y	E	E	S	I	L	C	R	X	K	D	U	R	B
L	D	F	W	M	J	L	E	X	H	M	T	B	C	T
G	W	A	W	L	E	K	J	D	X	P	Q	D	O	A
I	K	B	D	Q	P	X	D	Y	U	Y	R	M	N	M

DYFED	NOBLEMAN	PWYLL
FEAST	PRINCE	RHIANNON
GWAWL	PRYDERI	WEDDING

CROSSWORD: MYTHOLOGICAL BEASTS

ACROSS:

2. Giant ogre-like monster in Japanese mythology (3)

5. Has the body of a lion and head and wings of an eagle (7)

6. Blood-sucking demon goddess from Mesopotamian mythology (8)

DOWN:

1. The three sisters Stheno, Euryale and Medusa were one (6)

3. Headless horseman from Celtic mythology who heralds death (8)

4. Winged horse of Greek mythology (7)

TRIVIA

Who is the Roman equivalent of the Greek goddess Hestia?

a) Diana
b) Juno
c) Vesta

PAIRS GAME

Can you match up the 20 runes in 20 seconds? The first one has been done for you.

WORD WHEEL

See how many words of four or more letters you can make from the letters below. All words must include the central letter, and proper nouns don't count! Can you find the nine-letter plant which, according to Norse mythology, was the only one that could be used to kill the god Baldur the Beautiful?

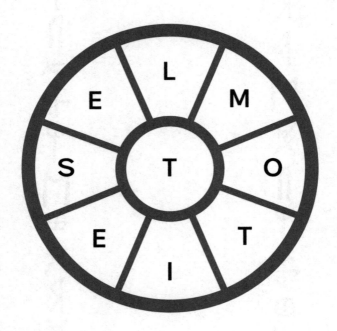

MAZE

Can you help the Egyptian god Ra to his sun boat?

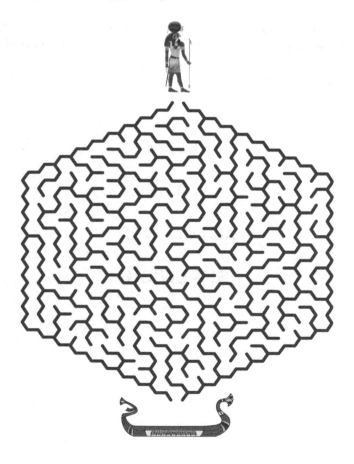

ANAGRAMS: SACRED CATS

In ancient Egypt, cats were considered sacred, and the goddess Bastet was human in form but had the head of a cat. Rearrange these letters to reveal words associated with all types of cats.

EELFIN

WOME

ACTUALWER

SHREWISK

WORD LADDER

Goddesses of love are everywhere, from Aphrodite to Venus to Freya. Here, can you change "love" to "mind" by altering one letter at a time to make a new word on each step of the ladder?

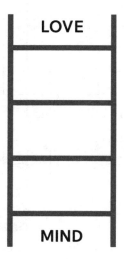

CROSSWORD: ALL THE WORLD'S A STAGE

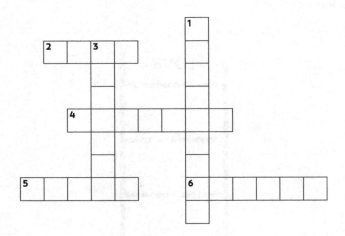

ACROSS:

2. A mischievous fairy or sprite from *A Midsummer Night's Dream* (4)

4. Three of these characters appear in the opening scene of *Macbeth* (7)

5. The Roman goddess who appears in *Pericles, Prince of Tyre* (5)

6. King of the fairies and character in *A Midsummer Night's Dream* (6)

DOWN:

1. Leader of the Greek invasion during the Trojan war in *Troilus and Cressida* (9)

3. Half human, half monster and occupant of the island in *The Tempest* (7)

COUNTING
CONUNDRUM

🏹🐴 + 🏹🐴 + 🏹🐴 = 24

🏹🐴 + 🐴🪽 = 40

🐴🪽 − 🐉 = 21

🏹🐴 + 🐉 + 🐴🪽 = ?

RIDDLE

The following clues will reveal the name of the person who, according to Chinese myth, was the supreme ruler of heaven, the Jade _ _ _ _ _ _ _.

My first is in beast, but not in fangs
My second is in Minotaur and also in monster
My third is in punish, but not in shine
My fourth is in creep and also in spear
My fifth is in sister, but not in insist
My sixth is in fortune, but not in free
My seventh is in journey, but not in honey

Who am I?

WORD SEARCH: THE ENNEAD

In ancient Egypt, the Ennead was a group of nine gods worshipped at Heliopolis, City of the Sun. Find the names of these gods in the grid.

L	Z	O	W	T	L	E	M	E	H	D	R	A	I	T
R	L	W	S	T	L	H	I	M	T	U	Z	S	Y	F
S	H	U	I	G	E	M	X	D	H	U	I	D	F	U
H	P	Q	R	E	T	F	D	R	W	S	N	P	X	D
Y	P	F	I	B	U	U	N	R	F	F	P	Q	E	M
N	H	R	S	J	I	V	W	U	C	F	H	B	B	Y
F	N	Q	O	G	R	L	Y	D	T	Y	G	Y	J	W
Z	H	W	D	Z	Q	J	Z	W	Q	A	I	E	X	R
L	R	R	F	N	C	C	X	P	J	H	L	Z	R	E
F	A	S	M	I	U	F	F	F	K	U	K	B	L	I
A	Y	Y	R	T	A	I	G	Z	F	J	J	N	R	H
K	T	U	V	T	S	C	F	M	I	G	Q	I	T	S
W	M	U	E	Q	F	L	Z	S	E	Y	S	Q	D	Z
Z	Q	S	M	S	Y	H	T	H	P	E	N	K	Y	M
V	V	U	B	Y	D	X	M	N	Q	N	B	G	Z	E

ATUM	NEPHTHYS	SET
GEB	NUT	SHU
ISIS	OSIRIS	TEFNUT

ACROSTIC

According to Greek mythology, this goddess was kidnapped by Hades to become queen of the underworld. Use the clues to reveal her name.

1. Stop sharply (two words)

2. Improve a life

3. Style of architecture using curves in particular

4. Miserable and morose

5. Horse-like

1.					
2.					
3.					
4.					
5.					

TRIVIA

According to Aztec mythology, when the four gods known as the Tezcatlipocas were creating the world, they came across a monstrous being called Cipactli, which kept eating what they created. What kind of beast was Cipactli?

a) A fearsome jaguar
b) A monstrous crocodile
c) A giant monkey

QUIZ: MĀORI MYTHOLOGY

1. Whakapapa is a key aspect of Māori mythology — what is it?

a) The reciting of a person's lineage and genealogy
b) The rhythmic beating of a drum
c) The noise of waves hitting a boat

2. Which Disney film features the Māori demigod Maui?

a) *Pocahontas*
b) *Moana*
c) *The Little Mermaid*

3. What did the character Ruatepupuke steal from Tangaroa, the god of the sea, to give to humankind?

a) Whakairo, the Māori art of carving
b) Fish
c) Fire

SPOT THE DIFFERENCE

Can you spot the five differences between these two pictures?

WORD BUILDER

The letters of a seven-letter word have been numbered 1 to 7. Use the clues to reveal the name of a female spirit, a harbinger of death in Celtic mythology.

Letters 5, 6 and 3 give the name of an egg layer

Letters 1, 2 and 3 give us a prohibition

Letters 4, 5, 6, 7 and 3 give us a patina or gloss

1	2	3	4	5	6	7

MYSTERY SUDOKU

Poseidon is well known as the Olympian god of the sea, but who was the Titan god who ruled over fresh water? Complete the grid so that every row, column and 3 × 3 box contains the letters A C E I N O R S U. One row or column contains the seven-letter answer.

		I				C	
	C	E					
		N			R	S		E
	I		S				N	C
	O					U		
	E		C				R	A
		U			E	A		S
	R	O						
			O				E	

BETWEEN THE LINES

The name of Virgil's famous poem that commemorates the founding of Rome by the Trojan hero Aeneas can be inserted in the blank line so that, reading downwards, six three-letter words are formed. What is the hidden word between the lines?

B	B	I	R	T	A
G	D	K	D	E	D

HIDDEN WORDS

In each of the five sentences below, a word associated with Japanese culture is hidden.

For instance, in the sentence "When I go on holiday to ski, Monopoly is not something I play", the word "kimono" is hidden in "**ski, Mono**poly".

1. Eating tiramisu motivated me to buy the cookbook.
2. We often guessed how many trains would pass Mount Fuji in an hour.
3. Do you know what the first emperor was called? Jim must know.
4. The woman gave the signal to go.
5. Shake the knee and shin to avoid cramp.

WORD SEARCH: THESEUS AND THE MINOTAUR

Find the words associated with the myth in the grid.

```
J  R  L  H  V  V  U  E  I  A  U  E  A  M  D
L  D  N  W  N  L  I  N  W  R  L  E  C  I  N
R  A  R  G  L  O  D  D  G  Q  J  N  I  N  U
T  U  B  U  N  C  D  A  C  R  E  T  E  O  O
S  B  B  Y  Q  Y  K  I  G  U  H  H  N  T  R
T  C  Q  P  R  H  I  R  B  C  G  L  H  A  G
H  F  J  R  I  I  R  A  S  T  P  Q  F  U  R
C  K  G  E  S  P  N  C  D  R  V  R  M  R  E
S  U  E  S  E  H  T  T  I  A  L  L  R  X  D
U  S  B  F  H  D  O  N  H  H  E  C  M  L  N
O  C  P  V  E  I  C  V  M  F  Z  R  V  P  U
Q  N  J  D  X  E  P  Q  T  P  W  I  H  J  I
W  W  N  Z  S  Q  L  S  X  W  G  U  R  T  Q
Q  J  T  S  I  A  G  X  P  W  F  Q  K  T  X
S  T  P  H  A  L  W  C  F  F  I  B  G  L  F
```

ARIADNE	LABYRINTH	THESEUS
BULL	MINOTAUR	THREAD
CRETE	PRINCESS	UNDERGROUND

CROSSWORD: SACRED FOOD

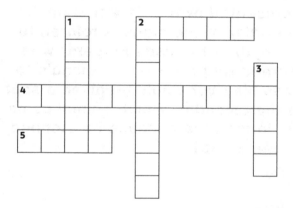

ACROSS:

2. Eris, the Greek goddess of discord, threw this fruit among the guests at the wedding of Thetis and Peleus (5)

4. In the Indian *Ramayana*, the monkey god eats the sun, thinking of this fruit (11)

5. Drink associated with the Greek god Dionysus (4)

DOWN:

1. The type of fish the poet Finegas spent seven years searching for in Celtic mythology (6)

2. The food of the gods in Greek and Roman mythology (8)

3. The type of fruit the Monkey King was told to guard by the Jade Emperor, but ate instead (5)

TRIVIA

The Chinese zodiac is a repeating cycle of 12 years, each year represented by a different animal. The order of the signs is related to the myth of the Jade Emperor who decreed that the first 12 animals to cross his river would be given a spot on the calendar. Which animal came last in the race because he stopped to take a nap?

a) Pig
b) Dog
c) Rabbit

PAIRS GAME

Match up the 20 glyphs in 20 seconds. The first one has been done for you.

WORD WHEEL

See how many words of four or more letters you can make from the letters below. All words must include the central letter and, apart from the target word, proper nouns don't count! Can you use all the letters to find the name of a Valkyrie who Norse god Odin condemned to eternal sleep, surrounded by a ring of fire?

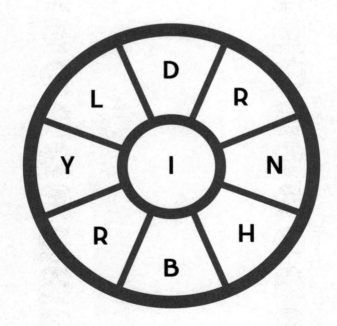

MAZE

Can you help the mermaid to her island home?

ANAGRAMS: ROMAN GODS

Rearrange these letters to reveal the names of some Roman gods.

CASH CUB

PUN TEEN

CURRY ME

ARM HITS

WORD LADDER

In the Greek myth, star-crossed lover Leander swam the Hellespont to be with Hero. Change "swim" into "land" by altering one letter at a time to make a new word on each step of the ladder.

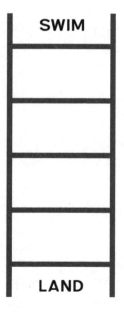

SWIM

LAND

CROSSWORD: PLANTS NAMED AFTER GREEK DEITIES

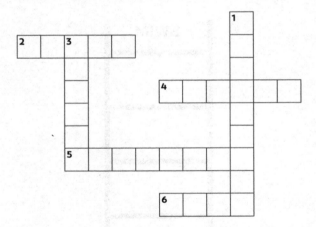

ACROSS:

2. Named after Paeon, a student of the god of medicine and healing (5)

4. A youth who was changed by the gods into a saffron flower (6)

5. Also known as carnation and considered the flower of the gods (8)

6. Popular showy flower named after the goddess of the rainbow (4)

DOWN:

1. Beautiful son of river god Cephissus who was in love with his own reflection (9)

3. Linked to the son of a nymph and satyr, who gave him a powerful libido (6)

COUNTING
CONUNDRUM

🐊 + 🐊 🦫 + 🐊 🐊 = 50

🐊 + 🐸 🐸 + 🐸 🐊 = 42

🦘 🦘 − 🐸 = 4

🐊 + (🐸 × 🦘) = ?

WORD LINK

The three words in each of the clues below have a word in common. For example, if the clue was "light", "screen" and "stroke", the answer would be "sun" (sunlight, sunscreen and sunstroke). Use the clues to reveal a word in the shaded column, a natural disaster the Mayan creator deities used to punish the first humans when they would not worship them.

1. Blood, style, guard
2. Door, blue, dumb
3. Fall, ball, flake
4. Print, bridge, loose
5. Home, ready, man

1.			
2.			
3.			
4.			
5.			

WORD SEARCH: KING ARTHUR

Stories about the legendary King Arthur and the Knights of the Round Table feature prominently in British mythology. Find the words associated with these stories in the grid.

R	Z	X	J	N	B	Z	L	V	E	V	F	N	M	M
J	U	Q	C	F	U	G	P	R	X	P	R	K	T	B
F	C	H	X	E	C	W	E	K	R	R	C	F	B	P
H	N	T	T	E	I	V	D	M	U	Y	Z	S	Y	C
L	C	L	T	R	E	E	A	G	B	V	O	S	D	Y
C	A	D	X	N	A	G	K	N	I	G	H	T	L	X
H	S	K	I	I	I	T	N	I	L	R	E	M	A	B
V	R	U	E	C	Q	F	N	S	A	I	J	C	N	U
V	G	V	I	Q	J	R	Y	V	C	Q	J	V	C	D
U	H	A	B	X	V	A	T	D	X	F	Y	R	E	W
D	N	A	R	H	S	M	B	X	E	T	Z	G	L	J
W	R	P	V	N	Z	D	H	M	L	S	F	S	O	I
W	A	O	W	Q	T	Y	W	G	L	E	J	E	T	S
Z	F	X	W	E	H	T	H	G	D	A	G	I	Y	K
P	H	A	G	S	Z	R	I	F	C	A	L	M	W	V

ARTHUR	KNIGHT	MAGICIAN
EXCALIBUR	LAKE	MERLIN
GUINEVERE	LANCELOT	SWORD

ACROSTIC

Use the clues to find words to write in the grid and the shaded squares will reveal the abode of spirits that is known across different cultures by different names, from Duat in Egyptian mythology to Orcus in Roman mythology. What is it?

1. Stream of liquid that goes against gravity
2. An official that diplomatically represents the Pope
3. A short knife
4. A mineralized surface
5. Having an unpleasant smell due to decomposition

1.					
2.					
3.					
4.					
5.					

TRIVIA

In Aboriginal mythology, the sun appears as a female deity called Gnowee. She climbed into the sky with a torch in order to get a better look at the world below. Who was she searching for?

a) Her lost infant son
b) Her unfaithful lover
c) Her mother

135

QUIZ: IT'S ALL IN A NAME

Here are three words and names associated with mythologies. Do you have the knowledge to pick the correct definitions?

1. **According to Hindu mythology, what are the Puranas?**

    a) A group of tyrannical kings
    b) Sacred writings on Hindu mythology
    c) Mystical, cloud-topped islands

2. **What was the *Popol Vuh*?**

    a) One of the only texts recording Mayan myth
    b) The protagonist of a Mayan creation myth
    c) The name of the apocalypse in Mayan mythology

3. **In Japanese mythology, who are the Tanuki?**

    a) Bioluminescent fish
    b) Mischievous raccoon dogs
    c) Spirits associated with the moon

SPOT THE
DIFFERENCE

Can you spot the five differences between these two pictures?

WORD BUILDER

The letters of an eight-letter word have been numbered 1 to 8. Use the clues to reveal the name of the Norse gods' watchman, who can see and hear all.

**Letters 4, 3, 7 and 8 give us a
place where flour is made**

**Letters 1, 2, 6 and 7 give us a word
that means return to health**

**Letters 4, 2, 6 and 5 give us a historical drink
made of water and fermented honey**

1	2	3	4	5	6	7	8

MYSTERY SUDOKU

Complete the grid so that every row, column and 3 × 3 box contains the letters B I J L M N Ö R S in any order. One row or column contains a seven-letter word that is the name of Norse god Thor's legendary hammer.

		Ö		M				
		N	L	J		B		I
L	B			Ö		M		N
	Ö						N	
I	L	J					B	
				Ö				
	N	I					L	
			N	B		S		
	J	R						M

BETWEEN THE LINES

Another word for heaven can be inserted in the blank line so that, reading downwards, eight three-letter words are formed. What is the word between the lines that best describes Aaru, a place in Egyptian mythology?

S	R	F	C	O	K	A	V
A	T	Y	R	D	D	K	X

MISSING WORD

Ma'at, the philosophy of balance and order, was the moral principle by which Egyptians lived. According to mythology, the goddess of the same name who embodied this principle would judge the souls of the dead to determine whether they could enter paradise. Fill in the blanks to make two compound words or phrases in order to reveal three words that relate to this rite.

Sweet		Break
Time		Up
Pin		Brain

WORD SEARCH: SEA MONSTERS

Find the names of some mythological sea monsters in the grid.

U	S	Z	O	J	N	P	B	L	K	N	V	B	C	B
O	Y	U	K	E	Ö	R	P	L	R	Z	E	Z	H	E
H	Y	D	R	A	D	R	E	U	A	V	V	R	K	S
O	U	K	I	C	O	V	M	S	K	C	B	G	I	C
A	V	T	K	X	I	K	I	U	E	S	K	Z	Z	S
P	U	N	W	A	U	D	I	E	N	Q	R	A	G	G
B	I	H	T	R	B	J	W	Z	Y	G	J	Y	K	W
Y	E	H	J	Y	Q	N	V	A	P	H	A	J	Y	F
Z	A	H	R	E	W	K	D	H	P	M	B	N	N	Q
N	Q	A	M	J	O	L	S	T	C	I	T	N	D	I
X	H	R	Y	G	Q	U	U	P	P	E	Y	N	F	R
C	H	E	R	J	S	D	T	G	K	H	U	N	U	W
A	L	L	Y	C	S	I	E	N	M	A	E	X	U	Q
Z	O	K	V	F	G	X	C	Y	I	S	G	Q	D	B
Z	R	A	X	B	V	V	X	H	Q	N	F	F	U	Q

BUNYIP	HYDRA	LEVIATHAN
CETUS	JÖRMUNGANDR	SCYLLA
CHARYBDIS	KRAKEN	SIREN

CROSSWORD: ANIMALS OF THE CHINESE ZODIAC

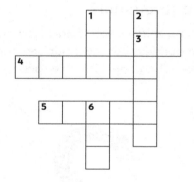

ACROSS:

3. Hard-working and dependable (2)

4. Enthusiastic, generous and kind (6)

5. Confident, determined and fit (5)

DOWN:

1. Kind, loyal and friendly (3)

2. Curious and fun-loving (6)

6. Quick-thinking, ambitious and not to be trusted (3)

TRIVIA

In a well-known Japanese myth, a woodcutter falls in love with a beautiful woman, but then discovers she is a jorogumo. What is a jorogumo?

a) A terrifying spider yokai (spirit) who lives in a lake

b) A moon goddess born without any bones

c) A shapeshifting dog with nine tails

PAIRS GAME

Match up the 20 shields in 20 seconds. The first one has been done for you.

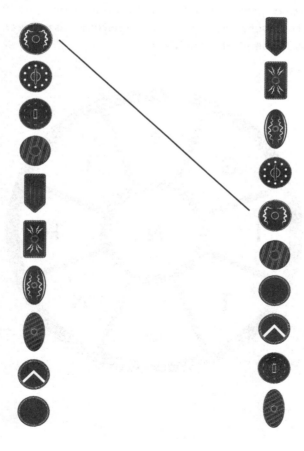

WORD WHEEL

See how many words of four or more letters you can make from the letters below. All words must include the central letter, and proper nouns don't count! Can you find a nine-letter word that precedes something associated with the gods Thor, Jupiter and Zeus?

146

MAZE

Can you help Heracles make his way through the maze to retrieve the golden apples in the garden of Hesperides?

ANAGRAMS: GREEK GODDESSES

Rearrange these letters to reveal the names of Greek goddesses.

ATROPHIED

DEER MET

AIM REST

PEER PHONES

WORD LADDER

In Mayan mythology, Lake Atitlan was where the gods of the mountain gave life. Change "fork" into" lake" by altering one letter at a time to make a new word on each step of the ladder.

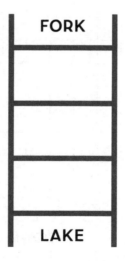

FORK

LAKE

CROSSWORD: ENCHANTRESSES

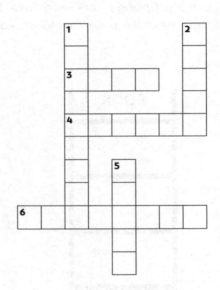

ACROSS:

3. Egyptian goddess of magic and healing (4)

4. Greek goddess of magic (6)

6. Welsh sorceress in Celtic mythology (8)

DOWN:

1. In Norse mythology, she was married to King Gjúki (9)

2. Greek sorceress who turns men into pigs (5)

5. Aided Jason and the Argonauts in Greek mythology (5)

COUNTING CONUNDRUM

$$\Psi + \Psi\Psi + \Psi\Psi = 45$$

$$\Psi + \text{⚡⚡} + \text{⚡⚡} = 41$$

$$\text{⚡⚡} - \text{🦉} = 9$$

$$\Psi + (\text{⚡} \times \text{🦉}) = \text{?}$$

MINI SUDOKU: CUPID AND PSYCHE

The myth of Cupid and Psyche is one of the great love stories of the ancient Roman world. Cupid secretly married beautiful Psyche, going against the wishes of his mother, Venus, who despised Psyche. Eventually Jupiter told Venus to back off, granted Psyche immortality and Psyche and Cupid lived in eternal bliss. Complete the grid so that every row, column and 2 × 3 box contains the letters that make up the word "Psyche".

Y					
	P	S			
C			E		
	H				Y
			S	P	
			E		

WORD SEARCH: MAYAN PANTHEON

Mayan mythology is made up of many gods and supernatural beings. Find the names of some of the most important deities in the Mayan pantheon in the grid.

```
F  C  N  N  I  Y  I  I  J  H  W  C  E  H  S
J  Y  H  A  P  I  T  V  X  U  Z  G  R  U  R
K  L  V  A  K  Z  Q  U  O  Y  T  N  L  N  O
J  M  A  T  A  L  L  Z  W  S  A  N  R  A  B
E  G  N  M  I  C  U  E  S  C  M  E  V  B  M
L  R  N  V  C  O  A  K  T  W  U  W  C  K  H
N  A  A  I  Y  Y  V  A  U  O  Q  Z  K  U  S
I  Y  U  M  K  A  A  X  S  K  U  T  N  Y  B
P  Q  N  P  B  V  K  J  W  N  Q  R  H  B  J
X  A  H  P  U  C  H  A  C  U  P  B  V  C  Q
O  S  N  S  S  X  G  D  C  E  Q  R  G  F  J
R  Q  F  G  I  T  Z  W  C  I  V  V  A  O  M
L  E  H  C  X  I  W  T  Y  K  A  C  N  K  E
K  M  H  C  Q  N  T  I  M  X  K  F  L  E  O
N  V  S  Q  P  P  C  F  F  L  C  F  H  W  T
```

AH PUCH	**ITZAMNA**	**Q'UQ'UMATZ**
CHAAC	**IXCHEL**	**XQUIC**
HUNAB KU	**KUKULKAN**	**YUM KAAX**

ACROSTIC

Use the clues to find words to write in the grid and the shaded squares will reveal the name of a reptile, which may have inspired the Japanese mythological creature, the kappa. What is it?

1. Liquid secreted in the mouth

2. Shrewdness, awareness

3. Myth, folk tale

4. Think highly of

5. "_____, _____ on the wall...", fairytale incantation

1.					
2.					
3.					
4.					
5.					

154

TRIVIA

In Greek mythology what were the Elysian Fields?

a) Birthplace of Demeter, the goddess of the harvest
b) Paradise to which heroes were sent after death
c) The site of the Battle of Marathon

QUIZ: THE AZTECS

1. **The Aztecs of Central America sought guidance from their gods by interpreting patterns in:**
   a) Coffee plant leaves
   b) Human entrails
   c) Animal bones

2. **The Aztec goddess Coatlicue was often depicted with a skirt made of:**
   a) Serpents
   b) Feathers
   c) Skulls

3. **What was the Aztec ullamaliztli?**
   a) An Amazonian god
   b) A mountain ruled by the god of rain
   c) A ball game

SPOT THE
DIFFERENCE

Can you spot the five differences between these two pictures?

WORD BUILDER

The letters of an eight-letter word have been numbered 1 to 8. Use the clues to reveal the name of a major Sanskrit epic central to Hindu mythology.

Letters 2, 1, 3 and 5 give us a military force that fights on land

Letters 5, 4, 1 and 7 give us a type of thread used in knitting

Letters 5, 6 and 3 give us a type of root vegetable

Letters 1, 8 and 7 give us the past participle of "run"

1	2	3	4	5	6	7	8

MYSTERY SUDOKU

Complete the grid so that every row, column and 3 × 3 box contains the letters A E O P R S T U V in any order. One row or column will contain a seven-letter word for the type of land overseen by the Greek Titan goddess Eurynome.

						S		
		A	T					O
				A			E	P
		P			U	E		A
T	V						U	S
O		U	R			P		
S	R			P				
E					V	O		
		O						

BETWEEN THE LINES

A word for prediction, the power which Cassandra was granted by the god Apollo, can be inserted in the blank line so that, reading downwards, eight three-letter words are formed. What is the hidden word between the lines?

A	D	B	A	S	H	A	B
E	Y	X	T	E	N	E	E

RIDDLE

The following clues will reveal the letters to the name of a Greek god and the equivalent of the Roman god Neptune.

My first is in creep, peace and also in spear
My second is in god, but not in dig
My third is in sea, but not in earth
My fourth is in eve and also in melt and hero
My fifth is in wish, but not in wash
My sixth is in bed, but not in boast
My seventh is in horse, but not in sheep
My eighth is in moon, but not in smile or lime

Who am I?

WORD SEARCH: STONE BLIND

In Greek mythology, the demigod Perseus sought to kill Medusa the Gorgon. Find these words associated with the story in the grid.

N	O	I	T	C	E	L	F	E	R	R	A	H	O	M
O	Q	L	H	X	L	Z	Y	V	K	O	F	O	C	V
N	O	W	B	L	L	Q	Y	W	N	I	Q	B	K	A
I	H	J	A	S	T	O	V	J	C	Z	Z	X	F	P
V	R	U	B	C	H	P	N	T	B	L	Y	G	P	P
N	O	Z	U	O	E	S	C	Z	S	A	Q	O	Q	S
D	Q	P	K	R	B	E	M	O	M	N	U	R	D	Z
H	L	M	S	B	A	K	I	P	A	D	B	G	J	A
R	M	E	Y	Y	K	A	H	B	N	D	E	O	Z	Q
N	U	S	I	L	M	N	N	D	G	N	A	N	Z	L
S	I	T	D	H	G	S	X	W	O	U	V	N	U	S
D	W	H	E	Y	S	O	Q	T	N	Q	B	D	A	Q
Z	E	U	S	T	V	S	S	C	A	L	C	P	C	E
G	B	V	X	N	A	T	H	E	N	A	P	H	D	D
O	A	D	T	C	K	Y	V	U	V	Y	J	V	A	L

ATHENA	PERSEUS	SNAKES
DANAE	REFLECTION	STONE
GORGON	SHIELD	ZEUS

CROSSWORD: EGYPTIAN DEITIES

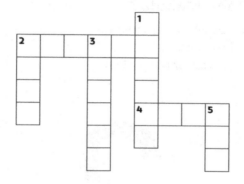

ACROSS:

2. God with the head of a jackal (6)

4. Goddess whose tears caused the Nile to flood (4)

DOWN:

1. The ruler of the dead, this god was the first ever subject of mummification (6)

2. The sun god, also known as Ra, who became Egypt's first pharaoh (4)

3. Goddess of childbirth, depicted with a cat's head (6)

5. God of storms and violence (3)

TRIVIA

According to Māori mythology, who was Tāne Mahuta?

a) The god of the underworld
b) The first human
c) The creator of humankind

PAIRS GAME

Match up the 20 runes in 20 seconds. The first one has been done for you.

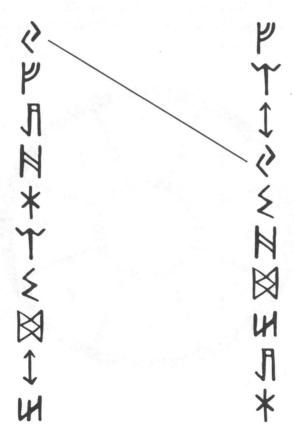

WORD WHEEL

See how many words of four or more letters you can make from the letters below. All words must include the central letter, and proper nouns don't count! Can you find the nine-letter word, represented by the Greek god Priapus, that uses all the letters?

MAZE

Can you help Greek hero Odysseus home to Ithaca?

ANAGRAMS: NORSE GODS

Rearrange these letters to reveal the names of some Norse gods.

DIAL HELM

LID VIA

DO IN

KILO

WORD LADDER

In Greek mythology, Zeus changed Callisto and their son Arcas into stars and placed them in the sky, where they became the constellations Ursa Minor and Ursa Major. Change "star" into "here" by altering one letter at a time to make a new word on each step of the ladder.

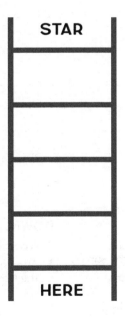

STAR

HERE

169

CROSSWORD: CELESTIAL EVENTS THAT INSPIRED MYTHS

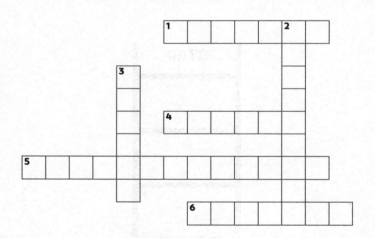

ACROSS:

1. Occurs when the moon obscures light from the sun (7)

4. Matter entering Earth's atmosphere (6)

5. Group of stars in a pattern shape (13)

6. When day and night are of equal length (7)

DOWN:

2. A particularly large moon (9)

3. Also known as aurora borealis, the Northern _____ (6)

COUNTING CONUNDRUM

🏺 + 🏺🏺 + 🏺🏺 = 85

🏺 + 🌿🌿 + 🌿🌿 = 57

🛡️🛡️ − 🌿 = 18

🏺 + (🌿 × 🛡️) = ?

RIDDLE

According to Celtic mythology, Prince Pwyll's beautiful wife trapped him in a bag. Can you use the following clues to reveal her name?

My first is in world and also in rain
My second is in heaven and also in hell
My third is in prince and also in bride
My fourth is in sea but not in sky
My fifth is in knife and also in knock
My sixth is in night and also in nought
My seventh is in over, but not in under
My eighth is in never, but not in forever

Who am I?

WORD SEARCH: THE *MAHABHARATA*

The *Mahabharata*, the longest poem ever written, is a Sanskrit epic central to Hindu mythology. Find the names of some of the characters and events in the grid.

A	C	C	J	Q	D	P	W	Y	W	U	E	R	B	Q
L	J	P	Z	A	Z	O	C	C	W	L	S	C	K	U
A	S	Y	D	X	N	L	I	R	F	A	R	A	A	K
T	R	A	W	A	R	T	E	H	S	K	U	R	U	K
N	G	P	V	U	M	I	W	A	P	M	C	Y	R	V
U	S	D	J	A	N	F	V	L	Y	B	Y	A	A	C
K	Z	Y	K	A	D	R	I	U	X	U	C	C	V	Z
A	S	Y	O	J	U	N	A	S	J	D	M	C	A	Y
H	G	L	F	D	J	A	A	T	H	Z	F	H	S	C
S	J	R	B	Z	Q	O	P	P	J	E	U	D	J	C
D	U	R	Y	O	D	H	A	N	A	V	R	K	M	T
Y	U	D	H	I	S	H	T	H	I	R	A	M	Q	D
B	V	N	U	B	D	W	P	F	B	D	S	M	A	R
I	C	V	T	A	W	Y	G	Z	O	N	D	Q	Q	N
B	D	V	Y	B	J	H	D	Q	O	W	U	O	R	G

CURSE	**FISHERMAN**	**PANDAVAS**
DURVASA	**KAURAVAS**	**SHAKUNTALA**
DURYODHANA	**KURUKSHETRA WAR**	**YUDHISHTHIRA**

ACROSTIC

Use the clues to find words to write in the grid and the shaded squares will reveal a word that means frequent earth tremors. According to Greek mythology, Gigantomachy, the eternal fight between good (Olympian gods) and evil (giants), resulted in these occurring in what is now Cephalonia. What is it?

1. Simple counting device
2. Instinctive reaction to pain or fear
3. Marking or pattern on skin
4. Glamorous or striking
5. Comment on or mention

1.					
2.					
3.					
4.					
5.					

TRIVIA

Which mythology is Richard Wagner's four-part opera series, *Der Ring des Nibelungen* (*The Ring of the Nibelung*), based on?

a) Greek
b) Celtic
c) Norse

QUIZ: CHINESE LEGENDS

1. **In Chinese mythology there is a supernatural being known as a Jiuweihu. What kind of creature is it?**

    a) A nine-tailed fox
    b) A golden fish
    c) A three-legged bird

2. **What is Chang'e the goddess of?**

    a) The sea
    b) The moon
    c) Creation

3. **Which animal of the zodiac won the race across the Jade Emperor's river?**

    a) Dog
    b) Rat
    c) Ox

SPOT THE DIFFERENCE

Can you spot the five differences between these two pictures?

WORD BUILDER

The letters of a six-letter word have been numbered 1 to 6. Use the clues to reveal the name of the princess who, in Japanese mythology, came from the moon.

Letters 5, 2 and 1 give us a wild ox with a shaggy coat

Letters 3, 4 and 5 give us an informal word for "man"

Letters 3, 6 and 5 give us another word for "happy"

1	2	3	4	5	6

MYSTERY SUDOKU

Complete the grid so that every row, column and 3 × 3 box contains the letters C E H I O R S T U in any order. One row or column contains a seven-letter word for a large bird, whose feathers are associated with the Egyptian goddess Maat.

O		T	R					U
C		U				S		T
			S			I		
			U	R				
		R			I		O	
			E	O				
			I			O		
E		O				T		S
S		I	T					E

BETWEEN THE LINES

The name of the first Aztec deity, who was both male and female, day and night, and good and evil, can be inserted in the blank line so that, reading downwards, eight three-letter words are formed. What is the hidden word between the lines?

T	I	B	S	B	I	A	E
Y	P	D	Y	E	N	E	F

CROSS OUT

Cross out all the letters that appear more than once. The letters that are left, reading from top to bottom and left to right, will spell out the word for a human in mythology, one who will die, as opposed to a divine being, who may live forever. What is it?

K	B	Y	G	M	C	N	O
N	F	E	B	X	R	S	Y
T	S	I	C	U	C	E	A
X	U	G	K	L	E	F	I

WORD SEARCH: DOUBLE TROUBLE

Twins appear in many myths. Twins in Greek and Roman mythologies include Romulus and Remus, who founded Rome, and rival twins Proetus and Acrisius.

```
T Z C A R A S G Q Z N M H V A
K S G Q P O T N X Q K G M H Q
S S F O E S M B I W B G Q Q U
E E L V G K A U N W F D E Z P
P L V U E Z J F L A T D E X H
O B H C A B A C U U E O Y B A
F Z H U C R E M U S S W R S N
F G O B R S I M E T R A U E U
D I O H I R U L X D Y T Y V H
Q T F U S L W T T N E F S A N
F A X N I Q G K Q O W W O N U
R Y A A U S R T R A P C K N H
R H U H S F L P V W A P B J U
N B E P V H D B X I X W K Q Z
Y L W U F D M X W A I N G W G
```

ACRISIUS	HERO TWINS	REMUS
APOLLO	HUN HUNAHPU	ROMULUS
ARTEMIS	PROETUS	VUCUB HUNAHPU

CROSSWORD: ANCIENT ATHENS

ACROSS:

4. Currency of ancient Greece and Athens (7)

5. Famous battle where Athenian and Persian forces clashed (8)

6. Athenian messenger and herald of the Gods (6)

DOWN:

1. Athenian philosopher and teacher of Plato (8)

2. Athena was considered the goddess of this (6)

3. Citadel built on a hill overlooking Athens (9)

TRIVIA

The Egyptian god Thoth, adviser and scribe to the gods, was often depicted as what kind of animal?

a) Ibis
b) Falcon
c) Ostrich

184

PAIRS GAME

Match up the 20 Celtic symbols in 20 seconds. The first one has been done for you.

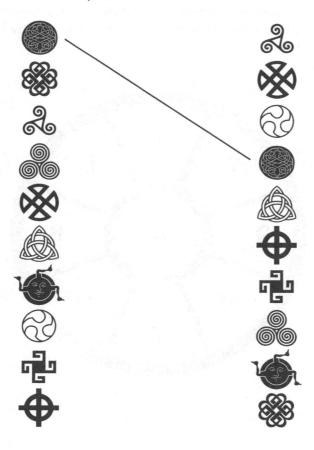

WORD WHEEL

See how many words of four or more letters you can make from the letters below. All words must include the central letter, and proper nouns don't count! Using all the letters, can you find the name of the structure where the Minotaur was imprisoned?

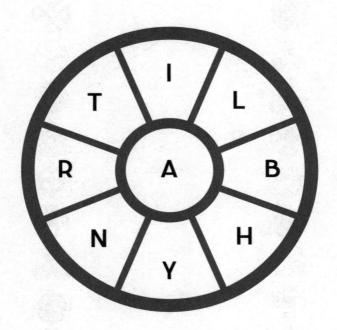

MAZE

Can you find your way through the maze from one Nazca Line to another? These were markings in the soil of the Nazca Desert in southern Peru, made between 500 BCE and 500 CE, and may represent deities or mythical creatures.

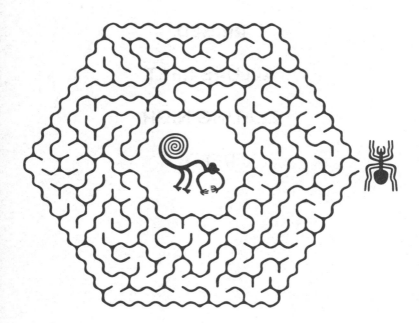

ANAGRAMS: TRANSFORMATIONS

Rearrange these letters to reveal the names of things that characters were transformed into during Ovid's *Metamorphoses*.

PRISED

ALLURE REET

ELATING NIGH

REED

WORD LADDER

"Mist" is an old Norse word for "cloud", but in mythology this is the name of a Valkyrie in the *Poetic Edda* poem "Grímnismál". Change "toad" into "mist" by altering one letter at a time to make a new word on each step of the ladder.

TOAD

MIST

CROSSWORD: TOURIST DESTINATIONS

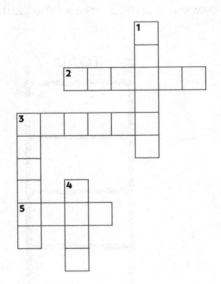

ACROSS:

2. Location of Aphrodite's rock (6)

5. Greek island, home of nymph Calypso (6)

6. City ruins found in Turkey and setting for famous Greek myth (4)

DOWN:

1. The Sagano Bamboo _ _ _ _ _ _ in Japan is said to be home to musical spirits (6)

3. The coast of Northern Ireland in Celtic mythology, the _ _ _ _ _ _ Causeway (6)

4. City founded by Romulus (4)

COUNTING CONUNDRUM

🏹 + 🏹🏹 + 🏹🏹 = 13

🏹 + ❤️❤️ + ❤️❤️ = 13

❤️❤️ − 🌹 = 1

🏹 + (❤️ × 🌹) = 42

DOWN THE MIDDLE

Complete all the following words correctly to reveal, in the shaded squares, the name of the Greek goddess of the hearth and home.

A	S		E	N
G	U		S	T
D	U		K	Y
L	A		H	E
C	H		L	D
F	L		M	E

WORD SEARCH: SCOTTISH MYTHS

Scotland is a land often associated with myths and mystical beings. Find the words associated with Celtic mythology from Scotland in the grid.

```
E  V  C  P  B  W  H  L  Z  T  M  A  S  H  Y
H  I  A  M  C  L  T  C  S  E  L  K  I  E  S
L  M  O  F  I  N  Q  J  N  Z  H  L  I  A  T
D  Z  I  P  G  U  P  V  Z  I  Z  P  F  Z  Z
Y  Q  N  V  B  P  R  A  X  S  M  A  O  N  C
Z  E  E  J  H  M  N  R  L  M  I  C  V  R  Q
Y  T  A  Z  Z  I  L  L  W  R  E  D  S  X  F
W  U  G  Q  U  L  A  R  Y  L  Y  E  R  H  T
F  I  B  I  J  E  I  C  S  R  O  R  J  Y  R
H  W  H  R  S  V  T  F  A  I  U  U  D  E  Q
N  G  T  M  O  H  D  F  F  H  R  R  O  F  P
V  M  Y  O  K  W  O  C  H  Y  I  S  G  O  I
W  L  C  S  Z  D  N  F  W  B  P  G  Z  Y  U
P  E  A  R  P  Q  E  I  P  L  E  K  U  G  U
B  E  A  N  N  I  G  H  E  F  B  Q  Y  S  A
```

BEAN NIGHE	**FAIRY**	**REDCAP**
BROWNIE	**KELPIE**	**SEAL**
CAOINEAG	**MINCH**	**SELKIE**

ACROSTIC

Use the clues to find words to write in the grid and the shaded squares will reveal a warrior hero (two words) in the Ulster Cycle of Celtic mythology.

1. A short, blunt stick used as a weapon

2. Heaven on earth

3. A spicy pepper

4. The punctuation symbol used to join two words

5. A small, dirty and poorly dressed child

1.					
2.					
3.					
4.					
5.					

TRIVIA

What was the name of the vessel in which the Greek mythological hero Jason sailed to Colchis?

a) Mallí
b) Toison
c) Argo

QUIZ: INCAN MYTHOLOGY

1. **According to the mythology of the Inca people in South America, what was the Coricancha?**

   a) A legendary temple with golden walls

   b) A snake-like beast

   c) A percussion instrument

2. **What was the capital city of the Inca Empire?**

   a) Teotihuacan

   b) Cuzco

   c) Chan Chan

3. **How did the Incan creator god destroy the first people?**

   a) He sent a great flood to wash them away

   b) He rained fire down on them

   c) He started an avalanche

SPOT THE DIFFERENCE

Can you spot the five differences between these two pictures?

WORD BUILDER

The letters of a seven-letter word have been numbered 1 to 7. Use the clues to reveal a Norse hero and warrior, as told in an Old English epic poem.

Letters 4, 2 and 1 give us a structure spun by spiders

Letters 1, 3, 4 and 6 give us a round dish or basin

Letters 7, 6, 5 and 2 give us a chimney or shaft

1	2	3	4	5	6	7

MYSTERY SUDOKU

Complete the grid so that every row, column and 3 × 3 box contains the letters A H M N O P S T Y in any order. One row or column contains a seven-letter word that is another word for a ghost, such as the gidim in Mesopotamian mythology.

	P						N	T
		Y	T				O	
		M			N			P
			N	H				Y
	A	M			H			
			O	S				N
	H			T				S
	O	N				P		
	S						Y	M

BETWEEN THE LINES

The name of a bird that in Egyptian mythology was an incarnation of the sun god Ra can be inserted in the blank line so that, reading downwards, eight three-letter words are formed. What is the hidden word between the lines?

O	A	P	A	S	E	A	C
F	L	N	P	N	D	E	T

QUIZ: CELTIC MYTHS

1. **In Celtic mythology, which god is portrayed as a father figure, king and druid?**

   a) Lugh
   b) The Dagda
   c) Aengus

2. **Who is the Celtic god of the sea?**

   a) Manannán mac Lir
   b) Moriggan
   c) Lugh

3. **Which Irish hero is famous for his great strength and defeating the Scottish giant Benandonner?**

   a) Diarmuid Ua Uibhne
   b) Finn mac Cumhaill
   c) Oisín

ANSWERS

1. Word Search: King Gilgamesh

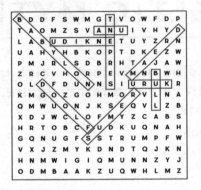

2. Crossword: Mythical Creatures
Across: 2 cyclops, 5 centaur, 6 mermaid
Down: 1 troll, 3 phoenix, 4 dragon

3. Trivia
b)

4. Pairs Game

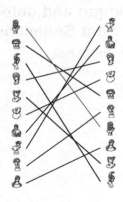

5. Word Wheel
Word that uses all letters = Aphrodite

6. Maze

7. Anagrams: Chinese New Year Celebrations
Lantern, firecracker, fireworks, dragon

8. Word Ladder
One possible solution: fire, file, bile, bill, bull

9. Crossword: Mythological Mountains
Across: 4 Apu, 5 Pangu, 6 Brothers
Down: 1 Chaac, 2 Olympus, 3 Buddha

10. Counting Conundrum
eye = 20, person = 5, ibis = 2, eye + person + ibis = 27

11. Riddle
Valkyrie

12. Word Search: Hindu Deities

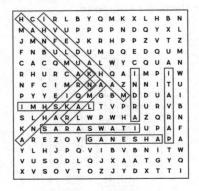

13. Acrostic

1 dahlia, 2 iconic, 3 spirit, 4 temple, 5 rancid. The letters in the shaded squares spell "distracted".

14. Trivia

c)

15. Quiz: Mystifying Words

1 b), 2 b), 3 a)

16. Spot the Difference

17. Word Builder

Lakshmi

18. Mystery Sudoku

A	B	W	E	O	R	I	S	N
S	I	O	B	A	N	R	W	E
N	E	R	W	S	I	A	B	O
I	W	A	S	N	E	B	O	R
E	R	N	O	W	B	S	I	A
O	S	B	I	R	A	E	N	W
R	**A**	**I**	**N**	**B**	**O**	**W**	E	S
B	O	S	R	E	W	N	A	I
W	N	E	A	I	S	O	R	B

19. Between the Lines
Carthage

20. Missing Word
Earth, dream, life

21. Word Search: Japanese Myths

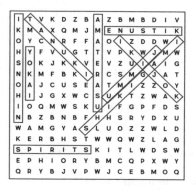

22. Crossword: Characters in Greek Mythology
Across: 3 Pandora, 5 Icarus, 6 Homer
Down: 1 Menelaus, 2 Jason, 4 Hades

23. Trivia
b)

24. Pairs Game

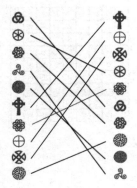

25. Word Wheel

Word that uses all letters = Polynesia

26. Maze

27. Anagrams: Scandinavian Sagas

Saga, hammer, warrior, runes

28. Word Ladder

One possible solution: moon, morn, more, mare, hare

29. Crossword: Words Derived from the Names of Greek Deities

Across: 2 nectar, 5 hypnosis, 6 Atlas
Down: 1 nemesis, 3 phobia, 4 Chaos

30. Counting Conundrum

Cross = 15, cat = 10, eye = 2, cross + cat + eye = 27

31. Word Link

1 pick, 2 sore, 3 seed, 4 bath, 5 peer. The word in the shaded column is "Crete".

32. Word Search: The Aztecs

```
T Q Q F T P N M X M J C M U J
E N M F E K A N S E L T T A R
S A E J G W B N F X H X S O D
G V G P H J T T X I D A U N O
Z H D L R J T X Z C N E A S G
F T C U E E L X H O T L K E N
C A C T U S S G K Z T D J W U
T O N A T I U H A I S V K L S
V X Q Z C Z D L T J D V T K W
J C W A O I C H M V T M U H
I T G F Y O C H E D Z E M C Y
K V R M A Y H G T M T Z O B
P A O T N O U O X U C Q L W C
J V L E E Q K T T H S Q J R K
Q B T N Q P K O D D A E H G T
```

33. Acrostic

1 abseil, 2 purify, 3 oilcup, 4 citrus, 5 advice. The letters in the shaded squares spell "apocalypse".

34. Trivia

c)

35. Quiz: Roman Deities

1 a), 2 c), 3 a)

36. Spot the Difference

37. Word Builder

Ganesha

38. Mystery Sudoku

S	O	P	A	L	Y	C	T	B
L	B	T	S	C	P	A	O	Y
A	Y	C	T	O	B	L	S	P
P	C	A	O	B	S	Y	L	T
O	S	B	Y	T	L	P	A	C
T	L	Y	C	P	A	S	B	O
B	A	L	P	Y	T	O	C	S
Y	T	O	L	S	C	B	P	A
C	P	S	B	A	O	T	Y	L

39. Between the Lines
Ragnarök

40. Hidden Words
1 goat, 2 snake, 3 dog, 4 rabbit, 5 pig

41. Word Search: Cheeky Monkey

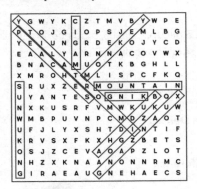

42. Crossword: Sacred Cities
Across: 3 Athens, 5 Mycenae
Down: 1 London, 2 Varanasi, 4 Rome, 6 Eridu

43. Trivia
b)

44. Pairs Game

45. Word Wheel
Word that uses all letters = Olympians

46. Maze

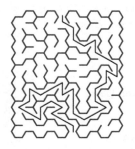

47. Anagrams: Egyptian Rulers
Ramses, Tutankhamun, Cleopatra, Khufu

48. Word Ladder
One possible solution: sing, ring, rung, rune, rule

49. Crossword: Mythological Norse Beasts
Across: 1 trolls, 5 squirrel, 6 dragon
Down: 2 ravens, 3 wolf, 4 kraken

50. Counting Conundrum
vase = 18, pillar = 9, statue = 5, vase + pillar + statue = 32

51. Riddle
Festival

52. Word Search: The Titans

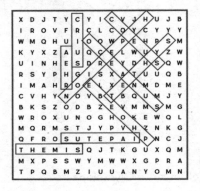

53. Acrostic
1 hubbub, 2 eraser, 3 advise, 4 retina, 5 tugrik. The letters in the shaded squares spell "heartbreak".

54. Trivia
c)

55. Quiz: Mesoamerican Gods
1 a), 2 b), 3 c)

56. Spot the Difference

57. Word Builder
Minerva

58. Mystery Sudoku

A	I	E	S	R	P	U	J	T
J	U	P	I	T	E	R	A	S
S	T	R	A	U	J	I	P	E
I	S	U	R	A	T	P	E	J
R	E	A	P	J	I	S	T	U
P	J	T	U	E	S	A	R	I
T	R	S	J	I	A	E	U	P
U	P	J	E	S	R	T	I	A
E	A	I	T	P	U	J	S	R

59. Between the Lines
Ancestor

60. Missing Word
Fish, sea, wave

61. Word Search: Dreamtime

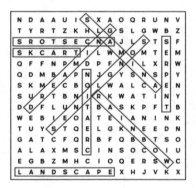

62. Crossword: In the Beginning
Across: 3 Brahma, 4 Pangu, 6 Tjilbruke
Down: 1 Pandora, 2 Ymir, 5 Aztec

63. Trivia
a)

64. Pairs Game

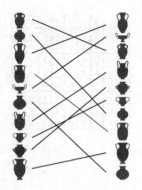

65. Word Wheel
Word that uses all letters = eponymous

66. Maze

67. Anagrams: Mayan Animals
Falcon, jaguar, rattlesnake, armadillo

68. Word Ladder
One possible solution: dawn, damn, dame, lame, lime, life

69. Crossword: Mythological Movies

Across: 1 Thor, 4 Atlantis, 6 Argonauts
Down: 2 Hercules, 3 Medea, 5 Troy

70. Counting Conundrum

Owl = 32, jackal = 12, ankh = 5, owl + jackal + ankh = 49

71. Mini Sudoku: Arachne the Spider

I	R	D	E	P	S
E	S	P	D	I	R
D	I	S	R	E	P
P	E	R	S	D	I
R	D	I	P	S	E
S	P	E	I	R	D

72. Word Search: Too Close to the Sun

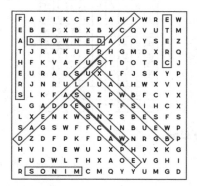

73. Acrostic

1 dread, 2 horse, 3 dream, 4 rhino, 5 Titan. The letters in the shaded squares spell "demon".

74. Trivia

b)

75. Quiz: Norse Legends
1 c), 2 c), 3 c)

76. Spot the Difference

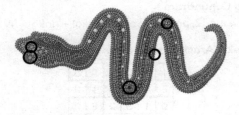

77. Word Builder
Artemis

78. Mystery Sudoku

T	D	E	A	P	N	R	U	H
H	R	N	E	T	U	A	P	D
U	P	A	R	H	D	T	E	N
N	H	R	T	U	P	D	A	E
D	T	U	H	A	E	P	R	P
E	A	P	D	N	R	U	H	T
R	N	H	P	D	A	E	T	U
A	U	T	N	E	H	P	D	R
P	E	D	U	R	T	H	N	A

79. Between the Lines
Sunshine

80. Riddle
Heracles

81. Word Search: Gods and Heroes

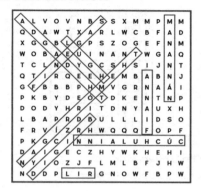

82. Crossword: Mystical Lands

Across: 4 Avalon, 5 Arcadia, 6 Aaru
Down: 1 Valhalla, 2 Elysium, 3 Jade

83. Trivia

a)

84. Pairs Game

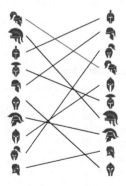

85. Word Wheel

Word that uses all letters = Hippolyta

86. Maze

87. Anagrams: The Underworld
Hades, Persephone, Cerberus, Charon

88. Word Ladder
One possible solution: poem, poet, pout, pour, sour, soar

89. Crossword: Sacred Trees
Across: 1 yew, 3 oak, 4 head, 5 Aztec
Down: 1 Yggdrasil, 2 Norse

90. Counting Conundrum
bird = 25, mask = 12, crocodile = 10, bird + mask + crocodile = 47

91. Down the Middle
Nephthys

92. Word Search: The Dagda's Harp

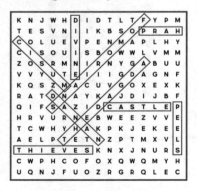

93. Acrostic
1 puppet, 2 relish, 3 obtuse, 4 milieu, 5 ethics. The letters in the shaded squares spell "Prometheus".

94. Trivia
b)

95. Quiz: Pangu
1 a), 2 b), 3 a)

96. Spot the Difference

97. Word Builder
Sekhmet

98. Mystery Sudoku

T	E	Y	I	N	Q	U	A	B
I	A	N	U	B	T	Y	Q	E
B	Q	U	E	A	Y	T	I	N
E	I	Q	T	Y	B	N	U	A
Y	**B**	**A**	**N**	**Q**	**U**	**E**	**T**	I
U	N	T	A	E	I	B	Y	Q
A	U	E	Y	I	N	Q	B	T
N	Y	B	Q	T	A	I	E	U
Q	T	I	B	U	E	A	N	Y

99. Between the Lines
Polymath

100. Cross Out
Wizard

101. Word Search: Prince Pwyll

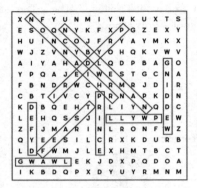

102. Crossword: Mythological Beasts

Across: 2 oni, 5 griffin, 6 Lamasthu
Down: 1 Gorgon, 3 Dullahan, 4 Pegasus

103. Trivia

c)

104. Pairs Game

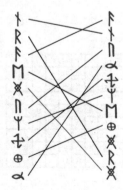

105. Word Wheel

Word that uses all letters = mistletoe

106. Maze

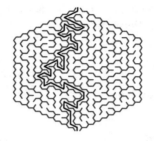

107. Anagrams: Sacred Cats
Feline, meow, caterwaul, whiskers

108. Word Ladder
One possible solution: love, live, line, mine, mind

109. Crossword: All the World's a Stage
Across: 2 Puck, 4 witches, 5 Diana, 6 Oberon
Down: 1 Agamemnon, 3 Caliban

110. Counting Conundrum
Centaur = 8, Pegasus = 32, hydra = 11,
hydra + centaur + Pegasus = 51

111. Riddle
Emperor

112. Word Search: The Ennead

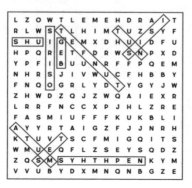

113. Acrostic
1 pull up, 2 enrich, 3 rococo, 4 sullen, 5 equine. The letters in the shaded square spells "Persephone".

114. Trivia
b)

115. Quiz: Māori Mythology
1 a), 2 b), 3 a)

116. Spot the Difference

117. Word Builder
Banshee

118. Mystery Sudoku

S	U	R	I	E	A	N	C	O
I	C	E	N	O	S	R	A	U
O	A	N	U	C	R	S	I	E
S	I	A	S	R	O	E	N	C
R	O	C	E	A	N	U	S	I
N	E	S	C	U	I	O	R	A
C	N	U	R	I	E	A	O	S
E	R	O	A	S	C	I	U	N
A	S	I	O	N	U	C	E	R

119. Between the Lines
Aeneid

120. Hidden Words

1 sumo, 2 tengu, 3 Jimmu, 4 manga, 5 Shinto

121. Word Search: Theseus and the Minotaur

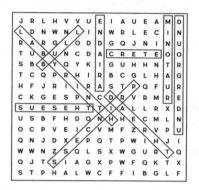

122. Crossword: Sacred Food

Across: 2 apple, 4 pomegranate, 5 wine
Down: 1 salmon, 2 ambrosia, 3 peach

123. Trivia

a)

124. Pairs Game

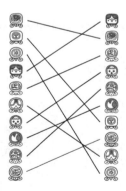

125. Word Wheel

Word that uses all letters = Brynhildr

126. Maze

127. Anagrams: Roman Gods
Bacchus, Neptune, Mercury, Mithras

128. Word Ladder
One possible solution: swim, skim, skid, said, laid, land

129. Crossword: Plants Named After Greek Deities
Across: 2 peony, 4 crocus, 5 dianthus, 6 iris
Down: 1 narcissus, 3 orchid

130. Counting Conundrum
platypus = 10, frog = 8, kangaroo = 6,
platypus + (frog × kangaroo) = 58

131. Word Link
1 life, 2 bell, 3 snow, 4 foot, 5 made. The word in the shaded column is "flood".

132. Word Search: King Arthur

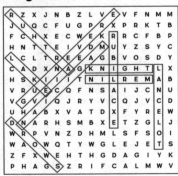

133. Acrostic
1 upflow, 2 nuncio, 3 dagger, 4 enamel, 5 rancid. The letters in the shaded squares spell "underworld".

134. Trivia
a)

135. Quiz: It's All in a Name
1 b), 2 a), 3 b)

136. Spot the Difference

137. Word Builder
Heimdall

138. Mystery Sudoku

J	I	Ö	B	**M**	N	L	S	R
M	R	N	L	**J**	S	B	Ö	I
L	B	S	I	**Ö**	R	M	J	N
R	Ö	M	J	**L**	B	I	N	S
I	L	J	S	**N**	M	R	B	Ö
N	S	B	R	**I**	Ö	J	M	L
S	N	I	M	**R**	J	Ö	L	B
Ö	M	L	N	B	I	S	R	J
B	J	R	Ö	S	L	N	I	M

139. Between the Lines
Paradise

140. Missing Word
Heart, scale, feather

141. Word Search: Sea Monsters

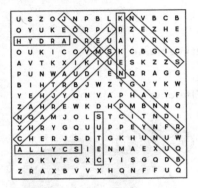

142. Crossword: Animals of the Chinese Zodiac
Across: 3 ox, 4 dragon, 5 horse
Down: 1 dog, 2 monkey, 6 rat

143. Trivia
a)

144. Pairs Game

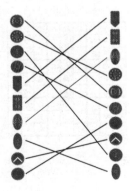

145. Word Wheel
Word that uses all letters = lightning

146. Maze

147. Anagrams: Greek Goddesses
Aphrodite, Demeter, Artemis, Persephone

148. Word Ladder
One possible solution: fork, fore, fare, fake, lake

149. Crossword: Enchantresses
Across: 3 Isis, 4 Hecate, 6 Ceridwen
Down: 1 Grimhildr, 2 Circe, 5 Medea

150. Counting Conundrum
Trident = 9, thunderbolt = 8, owl = 7,
trident + (thunderbolt × owl) = 65

151. Mini Sudoku: Cupid and Psyche

Y	E	C	H	S	P
H	P	S	C	Y	E
C	Y	P	E	H	S
S	H	E	P	C	Y
E	C	Y	S	P	H
P	S	H	Y	E	C

152. Word Search: Mayan Pantheon

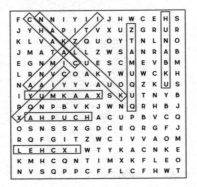

153. Acrostic

1 saliva, 2 acumen, 3 legend, 4 admire, 5 mirror. The letters in the shaded squares spell "salamander".

154. Trivia

b)

155. Quiz: The Aztecs

1 b), 2 a), 3 c)

156. Spot the Difference

157. Word Builder

The *Ramayana*

158. Mystery Sudoku

U	T	R	O	E	P	S	A	V
P	E	A	T	V	S	U	R	O
V	O	S	U	A	R	T	E	**P**
R	S	P	V	T	U	E	O	**A**
T	V	E	P	O	A	R	U	**S**
O	A	U	R	S	E	P	V	**T**
S	R	V	E	P	O	S	T	**U**
E	P	T	A	U	V	O	S	**R**
A	U	O	S	R	T	V	P	**E**

159. Between the Lines
Prophecy

160. Riddle
Poseidon

161. Word Search: Stone Blind

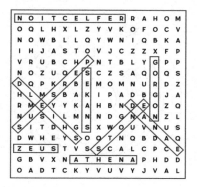

162. Crossword: Egyptian Deities
Across: 2 Anubis, 4 Isis
Down: 1 Osiris, 2 Atum, 3 Bastet, 5 Set

163. Trivia
c)

164. Pairs Game

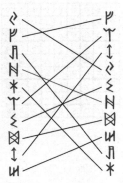

165. Word Wheel
Word that uses all letters = fertility

166. Maze

167. Anagrams: Norse Gods
Heimdall, Ivaldi, Odin, Loki

168. Word Ladder
One possible solution: star, sear, hear, head, herd, here

169. Crossword: Celestial Events That Inspired Myths
Across: 1 eclipse, 4 meteor, 5 constellation, 6 equinox
Down: 2 supermoon, 3 Lights

170. Counting Conundrum

Vase = 17, wreath = 10, shield = 14, vase + (wreath × shield) = 157

171. Riddle

Rhiannon

172. Word Search: The *Mahabharata*

173. Acrostic

1 abacus, 2 flinch, 3 tattoo, 4 exotic, 5 remark. The letters in the shaded squares spell "aftershock".

174. Trivia

c)

175. Quiz: Chinese Legends

1 a), 2 b), 3 b)

176. Spot the Difference

177. Word Builder
Kaguya

178. Mystery Sudoku

O	S	T	R	I	C	H	E	U
C	I	U	O	H	E	S	R	T
R	H	E	S	T	U	I	C	O
I	C	S	U	R	O	E	T	H
T	E	R	H	S	I	U	O	C
U	O	H	E	O	T	R	S	I
H	T	C	I	E	S	O	U	R
E	R	O	C	U	H	T	C	S
S	U	I	T	O	R	C	H	E

179. Between the Lines
Ometeotl

180. Cross Out
Mortal

181. Word Search: Double Trouble

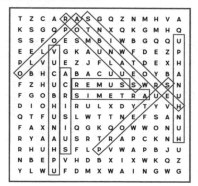

182. Crossword: Ancient Athens

Across: 4 drachma, 5 Marathon, 6 Hermes
Down: 1 Socrates, 2 wisdom, 3 Parthenon

183. Trivia

a)

184. Pairs Game

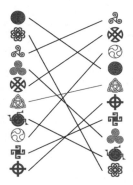

185. Word Wheel

Word that uses all letters = labyrinth

186. Maze

187. Anagrams: Transformations
Spider, laurel tree, nightingale, deer

188. Word Ladder
One possible solution: toad, goad, goat, moat, most, mist

189. Crossword: Tourist Destinations
Across: 2 Cyprus, 3 Gavdos, 5 Troy
Down: 1 Forest, 3 Giant's, 4 Rome

190. Counting Conundrum
Arrow = 11, heart = 9, rose = 17, arrow + (heart × rose) = 164

191. Down the Middle
Hestia

192. Word Search: Scottish Mythology

```
E  V  C  P  B  W  H  L  Z  T  M  A  S  H  Y
H  I  A  M  C  L  T  C  S  E  L  K  I  E  S
L  M  O  F  I  N  Q  J  N  Z  H  L  I  A  T
D  Z  I  P  G  U  P  V  Z  I  Z  P  F  Z  Z
Y  Q  N  V  B  P  R  A  X  S  M  A  O  N  C
Z  E  E  J  H  M  N  R  L  M  I  C  V  R  Q
Y  T  A  Z  Z  I  L  W  R  E  D  S  X  F
W  U  G  Q  U  L  A  R  Y  L  Y  E  R  H  T
F  I  B  I  J  E  I  C  S  R  O  R  J  Y  R
H  W  H  R  S  V  T  F  A  I  U  U  D  E  Q
N  G  T  M  O  H  D  F  F  H  R  R  O  F  P
V  M  Y  O  K  W  O  C  H  Y  I  S  G  O  I
W  L  C  S  Z  D  N  F  W  B  P  G  Z  Y  U
P  E  A  R  P  Q  E  I  P  L  E  K  U  G  U
B  E  A  N  N  I  G  H  E  F  B  Q  Y  S  A
```

193. Acrostic
1 cudgel, 2 utopia, 3 chilli, 4 hyphen, 5 urchin. The letters in the shaded squares spell "Cú Chulainn".

194. Trivia
c)

195. Quiz: Incan Mythology
1 a), 2 b), 3 a)

196. Spot the Difference

197. Word Builder
Beowulf

198. Mystery Sudoku

N	H	Y	T	P	M	S	O	A
O	T	M	S	A	N	Y	H	P
S	O	T	A	N	H	P	M	Y
Y	N	A	M	T	P	H	S	O
H	M	P	Y	O	S	A	T	N
P	Y	H	O	M	T	N	A	S
M	A	O	N	S	Y	T	P	H
T	S	N	P	H	A	O	Y	M
A	P	S	H	Y	O	M	N	T

199. Between the Lines
Flamingo

200. Quiz: Celtic Myths
1 b), 2 a), 3 b)

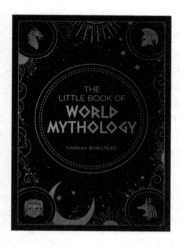

THE LITTLE BOOK OF WORLD MYTHOLOGY

A Pocket Guide to Myths and Legends

Hannah Bowstead

Paperback

978-1-80007-176-6

Step into a world of gods, heroes and monsters.

This pocket guide offers readers an engaging and accessible introduction to the major world mythologies, exploring their origins, foundational stories and key mythological figures.

If you're looking to enrich and expand on your understanding of world history, religion and culture, then this book is an ideal starting point.

If you're looking to enrich and expand on your understanding of world history, religion and culture, then this book is an ideal starting point.'Have you enjoyed this book? If so, find us on Facebook at **Summersdale Publishers**, on Twitter/X at **@Summersdale** and on Instagram and TikTok at **@summersdalebooks** and get in touch. We'd love to hear from you!

www.summersdale.com